The Street

For Maggie and in memory of Jimmy

The Street

Gerry Adams

Roberts Rinehart Publishers

Published in the United States and Canada by Roberts Rinehart Publishers,
5455 Spine Road, Boulder, Colorado 80301
Tel 303 530 4400

Distributed to the trade by Publishers Group West

ISBN 1-57098-132-9

Library of Congress Catalog Card Number 97-65654

First published in 1992 by Brandon Book Publishers, Dingle, Co. Kerry, Ireland

© Gerry Adams, 1992, 1997

Cover illustration by Proinsias Ó Coigligh

10 9 8 7 6 5 4 3 2 1

Typesetting: Red Barn Publishing, Skeagh, Skibbereen, Co. Cork, Ireland

Printed in the United States of America

Contents

Civil War 1

Monday Morning 9

The Street 16

Says She to Me 21

The Rebel 28

The Mountains of Mourne 38

Up the Rebels 58

Shane 63

Phases 67

Does He Take Sugar? 77

A Life Before Death? 85

A Good Confession 88

Just a Game 97

A Safe Bet 108

How Paddy McGlade Entered into a State of Grace 116

Granny Harbinson 123

Exiles 128

Of Mice and Men 136

Civil War

WILLIE SHANNON WAS a quiet man. He lived with his sister, Catherine, in the house they had been born in. Willie was seventy-three; Catherine was seventy-five. Until their retirements they had worked for two of the bigger shops in downtown Belfast.

Willie had been a storeman in Woolworth's, Catherine a buyer for one of Royal Avenue's fashion stores. Catherine could have become the buyer for an entire floor, "Silks and Lace"—Mr. Bradshaw himself had offered her the position. She had seriously considered accepting his offer but, as she would conclude primly to whomever she was addressing, it wasn't to be. She also had at that time an enduring but temporary attachment to a young man who had moved to Belfast from Banbridge. He was a Protestant and boarded with friends of Willie and Catherine's mother. He was a real gentleman, Catherine would recall, a little sadly perhaps, as she reflected on what might have been. She still had a photograph upstairs somewhere of herself and Ronnie, taken the day they had gone to the Glens of Antrim.

If Willie had tales of lost love he kept them to himself. He was fond of a drink. That was one of the legacies of Woolworth's. He had learned to drink as part of his apprenticeship. At first it was a bottle of stout, carefully nursed for half an hour on paydays in one of the snugs in Kelly's before he caught the bus home. Later, as he came out of his teens, he graduated to pints of porter and on special occasions to a half-un of Bushmills. On those nights, in the beginning, dinner was delayed until Catherine bustled in to announce that there was "no point in waiting for our Willie. He's with that crowd in the pub."

Their mother would put Willie's dinner in the oven or between two plates atop a pot of simmering water while Catherine served the rest of the family. There were two more in the family, James and Lily, who were younger than Catherine and Willie. James, to his father's delight, won a place in St. Malachy's College. By this time Willie was three years in Woolworth's while Lily, the youngest, was still at St. Mary's Primary School for Girls.

Then their father died. He died slowly and painfully the year James started in St. Malachy's. In a way Willie became the father figure, the head of the family. He was twenty-three years old. After a while pay nights became his late nights. On those nights the family had their dinner at the normal time without him. When he returned later smelling of tobacco and Guinness and full of good humor his mother fussed around him, serving a freshly cooked dinner on a tray instead of at the table. When he had eaten his fill Willie usually slipped young James and Lily their "pay" before presenting his mother with his weekly subscription to the family's income.

"I'm away up for a wash, Ma," Willie would say, "and then I'm off for a pint. I'll be in early."

"That's all right, son," Mrs. Shannon would reply. "There's a clean shirt over the chair in your room."

Willie never gave her any trouble. On Saturdays if he wasn't working he'd be off training or playing for the Rossa hurling club, then back home for a big fry of bacon, eggs, black pudding and sausages served up on a bed of soda and potato farls. If the evening was fine he and his cronies would dander up to Charlie Watter's public house at Hannahstown on the shoulder of Black Mountain. Then, as the dusk slowly settled in on the city below them and sea mists smothered Belfast Lough, they strolled back again, yarning and boasting and laughing as young men do. Sundays were family days. They went to early mass together. They ate well at noontime, a Sunday dinner which was prepared and served by Mrs. Shannon and her daughters while Willie enjoyed a leisurely read of the *Sunday Press*. After dinner he and James washed up the dishes and they talked of hurling and football or Willie would quiz James good-humoredly about his schoolwork. Then Mrs. Shannon and the girls went off visiting their Aunt Anne or cousin Mena, James settled down in the parlor to study and Willie strolled across to the Falls Park to meet his friends. In winter the routine was changed only to suit the weather.

It went on like that for years. In time James progressed through St. Malachy's and into teacher training. He got his first position as a trainee teacher in a small school outside Ardboe in County Tyrone. Two years later he married and he and his new wife moved to Strabane and from there to Glasgow in Scotland. Lily also married. She wed a schoolboy sweetheart who grew to abuse her. Their marriage soured as his drinking increased and their relationship degenerated into a behind-doors hell for them both, especially for her. Only Willie and Catherine remained the same. Their neighbors and friends, their workmates, the Rossa team, even Willie's drinking companions eventually settled into marriages, emigration and in one case the priesthood. Willie and Catherine and their mother persisted happily in routines which had constancy and reassurance and when Mrs. Shannon died Willie and Catherine carried on as they had when she was alive. They fitted into the rhythms of each other's lives. In many ways they complemented one another's lifestyles.

Willie was by now a senior storeman at Woolworth's and a committeeman at the Rossa club. One of the highlights of his year was the All-Ireland Hurling Final in Dublin. He would spend the weekend there, boarding in a bed-and-breakfast house close to Mountjoy Square. It had been part of his annual pilgrimage for twenty years, and on the Saturday he went there straight from the early train. He was treated like a king and reveled in the attention he received. Then, with a jaunty air he was off to tea in Bewley's, a browse along the bookshops on the quays, a steak dinner in Wynn's before strolling up to the GPO to meet the Rossa crowd at Nelson's Pillar. They all adjourned for a few pints and a sing-song in their hotel. No matter who won the match the weekend was always a triumph, and Catherine got a full blow-by-blow account of the game for nights afterwards. She knew every ween and turn of Willie. Sometimes she would tease him gently as he enthused about a particular action on the field or as he berated some player's incompetence. She, for her part, seemed content with her small circle of friends, an occasional small sherry and a regular trip to the theater.

She went to the Lough Derg pilgrimage every year; that was her All-Ireland. In 1967 she retired from Bradshaw's. After a month of boredom around the house she got involved with the local Ladies' Co-operative Guild. Soon she was enclosed in its circle of activities.

When Willie retired his workmates did a whip-round and presented him with one of the new black-and-white television sets. Willie was delighted. He spent the first few weeks of his retirement between the television set and the Falls Park. There was some sporadic trouble in Belfast city center that year. Willie and Catherine paid little heed to it. Indeed, if they hadn't had the television set they might not even have known about it. In the first week of October they went on a parish pilgrimage to Rome. It was there on the night of 6 October that Willie saw television coverage of the RUC's attack on the Civil Rights march in Derry the previous day. He was in a small bar when the strangely familiar uniforms rioted across a news program. He wasn't sure what it was or where exactly in Ireland it happened. In fact, he was slightly puzzled and then embarrassed when the barman drew his attention to the television in the corner of the room. "You Irish, you zed? Si? Look!" he pointed excitedly at the screen. When Willie returned to their hotel the group was talking about the trouble. One woman had phoned her sister in Derry. Fr. Crummey organized the phone call. The news wasn't good but the slight shadow it cast over their visit evaporated the following morning in the Roman sunshine.

4

"Isn't it wonderful how warm this place is on an autumn day?" Catherine remarked to Willie as they lunched in a small restaurant in the Via Flavia, a narrow street behind their hotel.

"Indeed it is," Willie agreed. "The Falls Road was never like this."

"You leave the Falls Road alone," Catherine replied.

The slight hint of an edge on her voice puzzled him but he took it in good part. Only when they were home again days later did he remember that little undercurrent of tension. It came back into her voice as they listened to a television debate between Civil Rights leaders and a Stormont government minister.

"I think they are only interested in creating trouble. Things aren't as bad as all that," she sniffed.

"Well, they're not that great either," Willie answered. "It's good that somebody's standing up for us."

"They're not standing up for me," Catherine retorted. "I'm quite capable of doing that for myself, thank you very much. There'll be no good come out of it. You mark my words. They are only in it for what they can get out of it for themselves. And the young people have no sense anyway. It'll be long and many a day before I'd need any of that crowd to help me. There'll be no good'll come out of their rabble-rousing."

Willie was surprised by her tone. They had never discussed politics before. He wasn't sure if Catherine even bothered to vote. He always voted but more out of some sense of responsibility than any ideological commitment. Of course he always voted anti-Unionist. And, he realized to his surprise as he reflected on Catherine's outburst, he had never told anybody about his voting habits. Now, with time on his hands, he was discovering that his attitudes were more questioning than they had been before. There was so much happening every other day, between protests and counter-protests, statements and counter-statements, all transmitted on the black-and-white television or reported in the morning paper. Willie found himself becoming absorbed in the political excitement of the period. At times he found it difficult to comprehend how Catherine avoided what was happening outside. Whenever he tried to talk to her about whatever issue was dominating that day's headlines she refused to be drawn into conversation. Things came to a head between them one morning. A man had been killed in an RUC baton charge the night before. The first Willie knew of the incident was at breakfast when Catherine flung the *Irish News* across the table at him.

"I suppose you and your friends are satisfied now," she cried at him.

He was dumbfounded at first and then as he read the lead story anger replaced his bewilderment. Crumpling the paper in his hand he followed Catherine into the scullery where she had retreated after her outburst.

"What do you mean?" he confronted her. "What do you mean am I satisfied? Them bastards kill a man and you give off to me? What do you mean, woman? What's in your head? I suppose it was that poor man's fault that they killed him?"

Catherine said nothing. She turned her back to him and adjusted the heat under the teapot on the stove. He flung the newspaper at her in anger.

"Don't ever say anything like that to me ever again as long as you live, Catherine. If that's all you think about the situation then keep your thoughts to yourself. And don't worry about breakfast for me. I'm going out!"

He didn't return until nightfall and although she had kept a nervous vigil at the parlor window awaiting his return she said nothing as he stumbled his drunken, hurt, mumbling way upstairs to bed. The following day she told him that it might be better if they didn't discuss politics in the house. He said nothing. The next morning he went to the funeral of the man who had been killed in the baton charge. He said nothing about this to Catherine and soon things in the house returned to the way they had always been, as if nothing had happened. But as their effort to avoid contentious topics of conversation intensified indoors, while the troubles outside continued to escalate, the relationship between brother and sister slowly turned into one of long, lonely silences. They were so much a part of each other's routine that the rituals remained unchanged, but as the awkwardness between them grew so did Willie's feelings of resentment and Catherine's sense of outrage. Gradually the warmth they felt for each other died. It was, as Willie remarked to himself one day, a bit like the cold war.

Yet he could not bring himself to make the peace: Catherine was demanding too high a price. He was prepared to compromise, to meet her halfway, but he was not prepared to surrender. It was she who was attacking him. Even a careless word from him about some incident or other was greeted by a scornful "You know I don't want to know that" from Catherine. Wounded, he would withdraw and a long, brittle silence would follow.

When he got drunk, which was seldom enough, then the resentment flowed out of him in an ugly, frustrated and angry torrent. He'd arrive home late and stumble noisily and clumsily into the quiet, waiting house. At first she used to scold him, rising from the chair where she waited anxiously for him to return, but his fury was so intense that she became a little frightened of him. She still waited up but now she held her tongue. Even then, in his drunken slyness he realized the power he had over her, and poured out his disgust at her, goaded to louder outbursts by her silent refusal to be drawn by his insults.

The next day he would be like a contrite child and for a while it would be like old times as he tried to please her by doing little things about the house and she slowly thawed, despite herself, in the face of his charm. At these times even the television news failed to divide them as they made a special effort not to let outsiders destroy them, but such was the daily controversy which swirled all around and so entrenched were they both in their views that such respites were not only infrequent, they were also short-lived. It was during just such a period, as they sat beside a roaring fire, watching the Sunday film on television, that a newsflash invaded their cozy contentment. Like the broadcast three years earlier in Rome the news this time, at first vague but becoming clearer and more deadly by the hour, was also about Derry.

They sat, numbed as the enormity of it was broadcast into their sitting-room. It was Catherine who eventually spoke.

"I'm sorry, Willie."

He made no reply.

"Willie. . ."

"I'm surprised you're not applauding," he exclaimed savagely. The wounded shock on her face halted him for a second but even then his pain was too great for him to contain.

"That's what comes from your creeping-Jesus refusal to face up to the way things are. Bloody British soldiers shooting our people down like dogs and all you can say is you're sorry! What are you sorry for? You've done nothing wrong."

He was on his feet, glowering at her. She looked up at him. Pain and disbelief were etched across her face. For a moment their gazes met, bewildered and hurt, an old man and an old woman in their own living room, brother and sister, spinster and bachelor, lifelong friends, and then slowly before his eyes she slumped from her chair with a little sigh and sprawled awkwardly at his feet.

She was buried on the same day as the dead of Bloody Sunday. Willie lived on, on his own after that. He retained his interest in politics. Indeed despite his age he attended the litany of local protests all that spring and early summer, yet he himself knew that the fire inside him had died. His sense of outrage had gone. He was, as he acknowledged to himself, only marking time. He died in August in the Royal Victoria Hospital while being treated for pneumonia. The hospital chaplain anointed him just before he passed away. As he did so the priest thought he heard him whisper something.

"What's that, Willie?" he asked.

"I'm sorry, Catherine," Willie sighed. "I'm sorry."

Monday Morning

A CANOPY OF WIRE shrouds the squat, grey two-story building. The entrance to the area between the wire and the building is a turnstile guarded by a security hut. Entry to the building itself—for there is no other reason to breach the wire—is by way of a double glass-paneled door which leads into a short hall watched over by two or three uniformed attendants. To the left are rows of dark plastic chairs; to the right another pair of glass-paneled doors opens into a large, empty room. Through here yet another set of doors brings you into a long, wide room. On one side is a counter topped to the high ceiling by protective glass. Behind the glass are low boxes of index cards thumbed through by mostly young men and women. They slip forms on request through openings in the glass shields to queues of mostly young, casually dressed men and women.

This is the dole, the "broo." It is a Monday morning. On the grey plastic chairs sit a dozen people. Some wear the uniform of the casually unemployed: training shoes, jeans, zip-up jackets or sports tops.

Other classes wear clothes like this, of course—occasionally. Many of the casually unemployed wear them all the time, at funerals and dances, at weddings and on street corners, in warm weather and wet. Some of the casually unemployed are women; more unwaged than unemployed, many are accompanied by small children. Prams are not permitted in the broo, though, so the small children thus liberated, or denied a resting place, laugh or whinge the time away, crawling over and under the plastic chairs and across the cold floor. Occasionally an adult or juvenile will raise his eyes off the tiled floor to smile or glare at the infant malcontents; others doze fitfully, one or two read newspapers, some converse quietly together. All are bored. When an attendant arrives with a list of names all look up expectantly.

"Grogan, McAteer, Russell." The attendant calls and the owners of the names signal their presence and are directed to small rooms or cubicles where they provide answers to the many questions asked to ascertain whether they can be permitted a loan or a small grant. Usually they wait for hours. Sometimes they wait for nothing.

In the big room with the long counter the signing-on is done. All signers-on go to a previously assigned, numbered part of the counter. They show a yellow card, a UB40, and pass over a white card which they have received in the post with their giro check—a new one with every payment. They are given a slip of paper in exchange. They sign this declaration which confirms that they have not worked since last they signed on, and that, usually, is that. At busy times a queue will form, at other times a signer-on may be challenged from behind the counter.

Occasionally there will be a spot-check. Is the signer-on impersonating someone else or are they really the person they claim to be? The large signing-on room is less grim than the smaller one. Fewer people sit waiting there, and unless they are challenged or spot-checked or waiting for a friend, most slip in and out as quickly as possible. Outside the building two streams of people moved urgently back and forth. Richard McCaughley, swept along in the human current, entered the building. A slightly built, dark-haired man in his

10

mid-twenties, he wore jeans, denim jacket and training shoes. His attractive face was unshaven and his eyes were cheerful and alert. He whistled quietly to himself as he went to his box and presented his UB40. He was shaken from his musical reverie only when the man behind him in the queue nudged his arm.

"She wants you, mate."

Richard looked up. The young woman behind the counter tapped the glass with her pen.

"Payment has been discontinued, Mr. McCaughley," she said. "I'm sorry, but you'll have to take a seat for a few minutes. Mr. Bryson will see you."

Richard nodded blankly. As he went to one of the plastic seats his mind raced ahead, panicking as the news sank in. "Your payment has been discontinued, Mr. McCaughley. Your payment has been discontinued."

He slouched into his seat. "What will I tell Jean?" he asked himself. He glanced anxiously up at the box. The clerk wasn't there. When she returned she smiled brightly over at him. Reassured, his panic abated. "It's just a mistake, some balls-up." They couldn't discontinue his payment. He had to live. He had a wife and two children to keep; they couldn't be left to starve. Indignation replaced despondency. "Who do they think they are? Treating people like dirt."

"Mr. McCaughley." A tall middle-aged man with glasses summoned him to the counter. He held a handful of forms as he leaned over towards Richard and spoke to him in a low, confidential tone which struggled to be heard above the babble of noise around them.

"Mr. McCaughley, my name is Bryson. Your payment has been discontinued: your oldest child has passed the school attendance age. If he is going to stay at school you will have to make a fresh claim. In the meantime I have arranged for you to get a special benefit. You will have to take this form to the lady up at special benefits.

"I can help you to fill in a new claim for your income support, or if you wish you can fill it in yourself and leave it back here for me." He looked quizzically over his glasses at Richard.

11

"What do you mean my son's left school?" Richard asked.

"According to our forms he is school-leaving age. If he wishes to stay at school," Mr. Bryson spoke more slowly and deliberately this time, "if he wishes to stay at school you will have to make a fresh claim. The claim for your wife and youngest child is being processed at present so I have arranged a special benefit for. . ."

"My son is only a child," Richard interrupted him.

Mr. Bryson's face wore the resigned look of a worn-out school-teacher.

"That may be so, but at sixteen he is at school-leaving age."

"Our Danny is sixteen months old, not sixteen years," Richard said tersely.

"Are you sure?" Mr. Bryson peered at him.

"Am I sure? Am I fucking sure? Of course I'm sure. I'm his fucking da, amn't I?"

"Well according to this form he is sixteen years of age and. . ."

"He's sixteen months. He hasn't even started school yet, never mind leaving it!"

"Well, obviously there has been some mistake. Can you give me the child's full names and date of birth please, Mr. McCaughley?"

Mr. Bryson noted down Richard's replies and went off with his handful of forms. He returned a few minutes later.

"Look, this is where the mistake is Mr. McCaughley; I'm very sorry. It's the computer printout."

He showed Richard the sheet of paper.

"I'll get this sorted out for your next signing-on day. It has to go back to central office, you see," he continued apologetically, "but you'll get the payment as normal for yourself and the wife and one child and if you go up to special benefits with this form you'll get payment for the other child. I'm sorry," he concluded sheepishly, "it's the bloody computer." He slipped the form through to Richard.

"It's okay," Richard said quietly. Suddenly he felt sorry for Mr. Bryson. He picked up the form. "I'm sorry for cursing at you," he said.

He turned and walked slowly out of the signing-on room towards the special benefits room. Mr. Bryson stood immobile behind his counter, blushing a little. Then he shuffled his handful of forms. He looked over to the middle-aged woman sitting opposite him.

"Spot-check, please! Mrs. Flannery?" he called brusquely.

The man sitting on the plastic chair beside Richard gurgled; that is, his stomach gurgled. He looked over at Richard.

"Was that you or me?" he smiled.

"What's that?" Richard stammered. He wanted to avoid conversation.

It was almost half-past eleven and he had now been in the broo for two hours. He looked over towards the cubicle. Somewhere behind the door his benefits form was being processed. His neighbor's stomach gurgled again. He nudged Richard.

"My guts think my throat's cut. I'm starved. Here, d'you want a fag?" he asked.

"Thanks, mate," Richard inhaled thankfully. He had smoked the last of his cigarettes for breakfast that morning. "I was dying for a smoke."

"Aye, I know the *craic* myself. There's nothing worse than having no smokes. Especially in a kip like this." He glanced up as an attendant called out a list of names.

"Nope. No luck there. Ach well, there's no use complaining. No point in biting the hand that feeds you, that's what I say."

"Unless you're starving," Richard observed dryly.

"Ha," his neighbor chortled, "that's a good one. Well said. Oops, that's me." He nodded over towards the attendant. "See ya, son."

"Thanks for the cigarette," Richard called after him.

"No problem, son. No problem."

Richard slouched into the chair and sucked his cigarette down to its filter. A slight nicotine-induced sickness turned his stomach and dampened his brow with sweat. He flicked the filter-tip away from him and looked about the room for a toilet door. There wasn't one.

"Excuse me, missus, do you know where the toilet is?"

"I do not, son. I do not indeed. I was just saying to myself, so I was, you'd think they'd have a toilet here. It's desperate. There's nothing here. Not even a place to get a cup of tea. I'm parched for a wee cup of tea."

"McCaughley."

Richard excused himself, stepped over two squabbling children and went, as directed by the attendant, into a small cubicle. He meant to ask the whereabouts of a toilet but when a small grey-haired woman bustled into the cubicle he decided to ignore his nagging bladder.

"Good morning, Mr. McCaughley; I won't delay you."

Richard nodded in reply.

"You're making a special benefits claim because your son has started work," she noted, glancing up from the paperwork before her. "He left school last week, isn't that right?"

"No, there's been a mistake. The man at my signing-on box is sorting it out. I'm having a special allowance claim in the meantime."

"What do you mean, a mistake?"

"The computer messed up my son's age. He's sixteen months; the computer put him down as sixteen years."

"Oh, I see. Well, we can't have that. I need a different form. I'll be back in a minute."

She rose and shoved back her chair.

"I've been here since a quarter-past nine," Richard complained.

Her face clouded.

"I'm sorry, Mr. McCaughley, but I'm doing my best."

"I know," Richard said sulkily, embarrassed by his tone. The door closed behind her.

"It's not your fault," Richard told the door. "It's nobody's fault. It never is."

Half an hour later he left the cubicle. An attendant was telling the dozen or so on the black plastic chairs that they would have to leave and return after lunch. Richard hunched his shoulders into his denim jacket and edged his way past them. He joined the stream of people bobbing their way via the glass-paneled doors towards the turnstile in the wire fence. The stream of people surged around and past him so that he was sluggishly towed in their wake onto the pavement outside. He went up the road and into the toilet in Daly's bar. As he left the bar a light drizzling rain started. He walked his way slowly home, a small, slightly built dark-haired man in his mid-twenties. His attractive face was unshaven and his eyes were downcast.

The Street

ASTLE STREET WAS QUIET. Mid-morning sunshine warmed the pavements and the shopfronts and created a pleasant, half-asleep, half-awake spring mood about the street. Sammy McArdle stood at the doorway of the bank. He had started as security man at the bank at the age of sixty; he was now in his second year in the job, the first regular, full-time employment he had ever had. He checked customers' bags and parcels as they entered the bank; it wasn't strenuous work and he enjoyed it.

Castle Street was a short, bustling street of high buildings, pubs, clothes-shops, arcades, a bank, big stores and a fish-and-poultry shop, and most days street traders hawked their wares on the side of the street. By now the usual opening rush of early morning customers was over. Sammy hadn't checked any of them: after all, they had been coming to the bank for years, since before he had ever graced its portals. On Wednesdays like this there were few strangers or new customers for him to scrutinize.

Jimmy from Eastwood's bookies had given him a tip for the big race and Big Gillen had stood for a minute or two with his bags of loose change, chatting about his bad back and the poor trade. Since then no one else had come Sammy's or the bank's way. Not that he minded: it would have been difficult to mind anything, he mused, on such a fine day. Even the British Army foot-patrols didn't bother him.

From the other side of the street Buster Traynor, the street-sweeper, shouted a greeting to him.

"What about ye?"

"Dead on," Sammy replied, stepping out from the shade of the bank's doorway. "It's a great day, isn't it?"

"Gorgeous," Buster agreed, leaning, arms crossed, on his brush. "It's well for you, nothing to do but to stand about all day enjoying the sunshine."

"Aye," Sammy laughed, "it's desperate isn't it?"

"And you're getting paid for it too," Buster continued. "Some people have all the luck." He started brushing the street again.

"G'wan out of that with you," Sammy chuckled. "You neither work nor want. A day's work would kill you, so it would."

"That's all you know. You and Cloop have a lot in common." Buster gestured down to the corner.

Sammy gave a wry smile: Cloop was the bane of his life. "You really know how to hurt me, don't you?" he chided.

"See you later," Buster smiled. "I can't hang about here all day. I'll send Cloop up to keep you company."

"Well dare ya," Sammy warned.

Buster continued on his way, pushing his brush and little pile of rubbish in front of him.

Sammy gazed down the street towards Cloop, who was sitting on the pavement at the corner of Chapel Lane. Basking in the sun, his back against the wall, face tilted towards the sky, he had one leg beneath him and the other stretched across the pavement so that pedestrians had to make a detour around him and his strategically placed cap. Cloop was a wino and he and Sammy confronted one another whenever Cloop set up his pitch outside the bank. Sammy was under strict orders to shift all loiterers. Usually Cloop complied with his request to move along but occasionally he was abusive, especially if there was anyone watching or if he was egged on. Sammy had given him a few bob once to bribe him to leave: the next day a queue of winos had settled outside the bank. That was the day Sammy's patience with Cloop ran out.

Sammy was a decent man. Life had not been good to him but he tolerated its inadequacies. He was by temperament a patient, pleasant, easy-going Christian. He had learned through a lifetime of little indignities to be dignified, to turn the other cheek, to endure. But he had rarely been satisfied; that had come belatedly to him with his job at the bank. It wasn't the wages: they were meager, but his needs were humble enough anyway. No, he just liked being employed. He liked the responsibility, the company, the sense of well-being, of belonging; he liked having something to do. He liked Castle Street, especially on mornings like this. But he resented Cloop. And now Buster was going to wind Cloop up and he was going to be tormented for the rest of the day.

Sammy glowered.

"Morning, Mr. McArdle." It was Mrs. Murphy from the holy shop in Chapel Lane.

"Morning, Mrs. Murphy."

"You don't look a bit well," she observed.

"Aw, nawh, I'm grand," he said quickly. "I was just thinking to myself about something. I'm great really."

"That's good," she concluded. "Such a fine morning. It's too good to be wasted worrying, Sammy. I'm glad you're okay." She went into the bank.

"Thanks, Mrs. Murphy," Sammy called after her. "She's right you know," he muttered to himself. "Worrying is a waste of time." He peered cautiously down the street.

Buster had gone round the corner without disturbing Cloop. Sammy brightened visibly, so much so that Mrs. Murphy remarked on the change as she left the bank.

"I'm glad you're back to yourself," she saluted him. "Keep your chin up."

"Right, Mrs. Murphy. Good luck to you."

"And to you too, Sammy. Remember, there's always somebody worse off. Look at poor oul' Cloop."

Sammy's face darkened. He looked towards Cloop, who waved cheerfully back at him. Sammy gazed past him, then averted his head and looked down Royal Avenue. When he looked up Castle Street again Cloop had shifted his position. He was moving slowly, still seated on one leg, edging himself laboriously down towards the bank. When he saw Sammy looking at him again he stopped and waved.

Sammy's face remained impassive. "It's almost lunch-time," he thought to himself. "The worst possible time." Lunch-time was when Mr. Timmons, the manager, left the bank. He would be going out the door just as Cloop arrived. Sammy sighed. It was just his luck, he thought uncharacteristically; it was going to be one of those days. Such a lovely day, too. He glared again at Cloop, who was slowly pushing himself into an upright position. He gestured to Sammy, then resumed his slow passage towards the bank. Sammy clasped his hands together in exasperation; he scowled down at the pavement and swung his hands apart. "Ah well," he thought, "nothing else for it. I'd better head him off."

Cloop was now almost at the bank's front window, but he stopped and leaned against the wall as Sammy walked slowly towards him.

"Mr. McArdle," Cloop greeted him. "Mr. McArdle, I was just sitting down there enjoying the sun."

Sammy glared sullenly at him.

"I was just relaxing there with not a care in the world."

Sammy stopped before him.

"And I looked up here and here you were all on your own-i-oh. Now don't worry," he said, anticipating Sammy's next move. "Don't worry, Mr. McArdle, you won't have to move me today. Nawh, that's not why I came up here. You just looked so alone and so worried lookin'." Cloop shoved his hand into the pocket of his tattered coat. "So I just said to myself: it's not fair me sitting here without a worry in the world and Mr. McArdle up there like all belonging to him was dead. So I brought you up a wee smoke, so I did." Cloop drew his hand from his pocket. His fingers clutched the butt of a cigarette and a whole one. He put the butt in his mouth and pointed the other one at Sammy.

"Here you are now. Give's a light and I'll leave you in peace."

Sammy looked at him. He looked past the cigarettes and Cloop's outstretched hand; he looked beyond his unshaved face. He looked along Castle Street and sighed. In the sunlight a shop window winked at him.

"Okay, Mr. McArdle?" Cloop asked. "You really shouldn't let things get you down. Especially on such a nice day. Here, have a smoke."

Says She to Me

S HE NEVER HAD her sorrows to seek. That's what I say. She always had it hard, so she did, even when others were getting it easy."

"Ach, I wouldn't altogether agree with that, Maisie. Like, I'm the first to admit that she never got it aisy but then who did? Who around here did? Answer me that?"

"Nobody did, but some got it harder than others and Lily was one of them, so she was. Sure you know that yourself, Aggie. You saw the way she was brought up. Her poor mother didn't get much help from oul' Davy."

"She couldn't keep him out of the bloody pub!"

"And was that her fault? Was it? Aggie, sometimes you get on my wick! You'd think the rest of us married saints, so you would, to hear the way you talk. Let oul' Davy rest in peace. He did more harm to himself than he did to anybody else, and even if he did spend a lot of time in the pub we know that he wasn't on his own. There was always plenty there to keep him company, so there was. Drink was his problem all right, but one thing I'll say for him: drunk or sober he never lifted his hand to her or the children. How many could say that about their man these days?"

"Maybe that's what Lily needed. Spare the rod and spoil the child. That's a true saying if ever there was one. No man ever has the right to lift his hand to any woman, but a child needs to be taught wrong from right, so it does. I'm not saying anything about oul' Davy or Missus Caldwell, God rest their souls. Or Lily either for that matter. I'm only making the point that there was no excuse for the way Lily got on when she was young. To look at her today you'd think she was somebody."

"Ach, I wouldn't say that."

"That's 'cos you don't know the half of it. You were always too soft, so you were. You look back on things now and you see them all nice and rosy. Well it wasn't like that, Maisie, so it wasn't, as you should know."

"Nobody knows it better. Do you think I'm doting? I was here, Aggie, so I was. I could write a book about it. I don't need to be told how tough things were. I'm trying to forget the hard times. Jesus, Mary and Joseph, if you went round all the time thinking of all the things wrong in this world you'd go mental. You want to be more positive, so you do. You need to get a good grip on yourself, Aggie love."

"Ach, I'm all right, Maisie. It's just that I met that Lily one down the town the day, so I did, and she walked right past me as if I wasn't there."

"Maybe she didn't see you!"

"Oh she saw me, she did. Says I to her, 'Hullo Lily' and says she to me, 'Hullo Aggie' and that was it. Before I could get another word out she was gone. She had a wee grandson with her: he was in her arms. She nearly knocked me down to get by."

"Well, maybe she had other things on her mind. There's many a time I be walking about in a trance thinking or worrying about this, that or the other thing, and if the Angel Gabriel himself appeared to me I swear I wouldn't take him under my notice. Maybe that's the way Lily was."

"That's you all over, so it is. Making excuses again. You'll never change, Maisie. Especially as far as Lily's concerned."

"Aggie, look, hang on a wee minute. You seem to have a bee in your bonnet over Lily Caldwell. Well maybe I know a wee bit more about Lily than most people, so if you houl' on till I pour the two of us this wee mouthful of tea, I'll soon give you the gist of why I've a bit of time for her."

"You could tell me nothing I don't already know, Maisie. The whole world knows she was fond of a bit of the other and that's the height of it!"

"Is that right now, Aggie? That shows how much you know, so it does! Here, take this cup off me. I'm scalded, so I am. There . . . that's better. Will you have a wee piece of cake? I've nothing in. You should have come next week. That's my pension week; this is my bad week. Here, take a piece."

"No, Maisie, no: I've to make me dinner when I get home. A cup in my hand is just lovely. Have you got your own?"

"Aye, Aggie, now where was I? Aye! You were wanting to know about Lily. Well, me and her were very close as you know. She was a few years older than me. She was working in the mill and we met through the camogie. I was still at school but we both got a wee job, so we did, working together at nights for a couple of hours in Mr. Keenan's sweetie shop."

"Poor old Mr. Keenan, now he was a proper gentleman. I remember. . ."

"Lily always got the boys. I recall one time saying to my mammy about, you know, Lily always getting the boys and my mammy said to me not to worry, she wouldn't have her sorrows to seek. Anyway, not long after that Lily got pregnant. She never told any of us, none of her friends or family. I didn't know until she was about six months and by then some of the women in the mill had advised her how to get rid of it. That's what the story was anyway. I couldn't tell you if it was true or not, Lily never talked about it. Anyway, she's supposed to have taken things to make the baby come away. If she did it never worked. The baby was born: it was a wee girl—deformed so it was; it lived for about a month. Poor Lily never saw it."

"Ach, I never knew that, Maisie."

"I know, Aggie. You were away at the time. Do you remember? You went off to Cushendall with our Aunt Sadie for the summer. You were too young anyway. Remember, there's ten years between us. That mightn't be much at our age now but it's a lot when you're younger, so it is."

"What age were you then?"

"I was about fifteen and Lily would have been about nineteen or twenty-odd. Everybody was talking about her at the time. All the boys at the corner arguing and saying it wasn't theirs. That really annoyed me. Poor Lily. And all the fellas she was so crazy about: all they could think about was themselves."

"Typical bloody men. They're all the bloody same."

"I still knocked round with Lily. Remember oul' Missus Reid? She came around one day and told me mammy that she shouldn't let me go around with Lily 'cos Lily had such a bad name. She was shown the door—nicely of course. Me Ma said that I was her rearing, not meaning any harm on Lily's mammy of course, and I could keep my own company. Like, me Ma wouldn't let you say a word about Lily. Lily was more often in our house than she was in her own."

"Is it true that her mother used to follow her about the place?"

"Aye, but only because she was worrying for her. Me mammy says Lily had a wee want in her, a wee weakness, and her mother knew this. I think it got worse after she lost the child. I remember hearing her mammy and ours talking one day and her mammy was saying that when you lose a child like that you have a wee craving inside you for another one. When I asked me Ma about it afterwards she told me I'd understand when I got older."

"Who was the father?"

"Nobody knows. Except Lily, of course. I heard years later it was a married man from Leeson Street. Lily's mother always blamed poor Sean Dunne from one of the Rock streets. Sean was as innocent as a baby himself but Lily's mother gave him dog's abuse. She never gave him the light of day, shouting at him in the street and this, that and the other thing."

"I never heard of him."

"Ach, you'd know his sister, Gonne. She married into the Quinns from Hawthorn Street."

"Ah yes, I know who you mean. Gonne and me were in the same class together. She never mentioned a brother, Sean. There was Brendan and Hugh and. . . "

"Sean ended up going off to sea, so he did. He's dead now, God rest him. He died in Norway or one of them places. Anyway, a year or so later Lily was pregnant again. Only this time she told everybody and her family and all of us helped her, so we did. The only thing was the fella she said was the one that done it: he said it wasn't him."

"Typical! Was he married too?"

"No, not at that time. I might as well tell you his name. It was big Sammy Mallon."

"Big Sammy? Nora McCluskey's man? Him?"

"Aye, he was a fly man in them days. All the girls were dying about him, so they were. Like, I don't know what they saw in him. It was said if you spat in the street you were bound to hit one of his children. But he denied making Lily pregnant."

"And did he?"

"Of course he did. Lily thought the sun rose and shone on him. She would have done anything to get him. Like I said before, she was a wee bit foolish that way. Sure he wasn't fit to clean her arse. He was the road to no-town. He actually came round to see me, so he did; he was never short on cheek. He knew Lily and I were very close. He swore to me it wasn't his child, that he hadn't been seeing Lily for over four months. I told him that I had seen the two of them together on Halloween night, which is the night she conceived, and he got all flustered. He said it couldn't a been him 'cos he was too big to go into her. Ha! The cheek of him!"

"Big Dick!"

"Aye. Or so he thought. I didn't even know what he was talking about. Then he told me that he had an operation and he couldn't have any children. I threw him out."

"You did right."

"That's not the end of it. His mother went to see the priest and the priest sent for Lily. She went down on her own; she wouldn't take anyone with her. I wanted to go but she wouldn't let me. I met her when she came back and she was crying. She said the priest did everything but call her a hoor. He said it couldn't be Sammy's child, that Sammy came from a good family. Then he came out with all the oul' shite about Sammy not being able to have children on account of the operation. Like, everybody knew it was Sammy. He had even been boasting about doing it before it turned out Lily was pregnant."

"You couldn't trust a man as far as you could throw him. That's a true say. . . ."

"Anyway, Lily had the child. A wee boy. A lovely child. You'd think big Sammy spat him out of his mouth, you would. He never ever acknowledged the child, not then, not now. He never acknowledged Lily either for that matter. That child fathered himself."

"God bless him. The street reared the poor wee soul."

"Sammy's father, by the way, he always knew that Lily's son was his grandchild. He wouldn't have passed him. Sammy himself got married a couple of years later. Within eleven months his wife had a baby and another one a year after."

"So much for his so-called operation."

"Any excuse will do. Fifteen years later Sammy's mother apologized to Lily. A bit late, but there you are. Lily just said, 'That's all right, Missus Mallon,' as nice as ninepence."

"She did right."

"Anyway, Aggie, that's the story of poor Lily. Now she's a granny just like the two of us. And you know something: isn't it sad after all this time that her past is still following her around, and her that never did harm to anyone."

"And never a word about Sammy Mallon."

"Or the married man from Leeson Street."

"It's a man's world, Maisie."

"Indeed it is, Aggie. That's as good a reason as any why we women have to be a wee bit soft with one another sometimes."

"But not all the time, Maisie."

"Indeed not. But I'll always remember what our mother said to old Missus Reid that time she came round. 'Never talk about anyone's children,' says she, 'when you're rearing children of your own.'

"Here, give me your cup and I'll fill it up for you. You know a funny thing? Ever since her son was born, and that's nearly forty years ago, Lily's never been with another man. They used and abused her and when they wouldn't treat her right she just gave up on them, and gave her life to her son. Now, all this time later, maybe she's got what she always wanted—a bit of love and affection and dignity."

"How would she get that now, Maisie?"

"From her grandson, Aggie, from her grandson. Everybody loves a granny, Aggie. Don't they?"

The Rebel

MARGARET BECAME A REBEL when she was fifty-three years old. She remembers exactly when it happened. It was July 2, 1970, at about half-past two in the afternoon. Up until then Margaret had been no more rebellious than anybody else. She was a cheerful, witty little woman with a family of five boys and four girls. Margaret's husband, a tall, stern-looking man, didn't get too involved with rearing the children. That's not to say that he neglected his paternal duties; on the contrary, he was a dutiful father. But he was a father of the old school, Victorian to a degree in his attitudes, working hard always to keep his family fed, and strict in the administration of discipline.

He had been a rebel once, in his younger days. Only Margaret knew if he retained any of that instinct or whether his paternal responsibilities had smothered it. It can be hard to be a rebel with so many mouths to feed and so many bodies to clothe. That was Margaret's preoccupation also and ironically that's what led indirectly to her becoming a rebel.

Margaret's son Tommy was arrested on the night of July 1 and brought to Townhall Street RUC station for an overnight stay before a court appearance on a charge of riotous behavior the following day.

Margaret received this news with some shock when Sean Healy, one of Tommy's friends, arrived breathless and excited at her front door with the tidings. She didn't know what way to turn, and when her husband came in later she was relieved that he knew precisely what had to be done.

"Give me my dinner, mother, please. First things first," he told her a little testily when she greeted him with the dramatic news.

Later, as he settled himself in his chair by the fire, he delivered his judgment.

"That young Healy lad isn't too reliable. I think you or one of the girls should go down to Mrs. Sharpe's and phone the barracks. That way we'll know where we stand. And if it's true, well then a night in the cells will do our Tommy no harm, mother, so don't be worrying. There's nothing we can do about it tonight except phone." He paused for a moment. "You'll have to go to the courts in the morning if he is arrested and," he reflected a moment, "we'll probably need a solicitor. Bloody fool, our Tommy. Go on, mother, go down and find out what's what, like a good woman."

Margaret said nothing. She was glad to get out of the house. Teresa went with her to Mrs. Sharpe's.

"M'da's a geg," Teresa sniffed indignantly as they hurried along the street, "he sits there like Lord Muck giving his orders. You're too soft, Ma."

"Oh, don't mind your father. That's just his way. He's as worried about our Tommy as we are. He just finds it hard to show his feelings. Here we are now. You phone for me, Teresa. I'll go in the back with Mrs. Sharpe. Okay, love?"

Later that night while the rest of the family were asleep, Margaret lay in bed beside the still form of her husband and sobbed a little into her pillow.

The following morning, with children and father dispatched to work and school, she and Mrs. Sharpe made their way to the Petty

Sessions. Neither of them had ever been in court before and they were unprepared for the babble of noise, the heavily-armed RUC men and women, the multitudes of people and the crowded confusion in the large foyer of the court building. They stood timorously until Mrs. Sharpe noticed a section of the crowd milling around a notice-board.

"Wait here, dear, till I see what that is," she said.

Margaret watched anxiously as Mrs. Sharpe disappeared into the notice-board scrum. She reemerged victorious seconds later.

"Your Tommy's in Court Number Three. Here it is here," she pointed to one of the doors leading off from the foyer. They pushed their way between the heavy swinging doors and into the cool quietness of Court Number Three. There they sat silently for two and a half hours.

Then the court rose for lunch. There was no sign of Tommy. Margaret was beside herself with anxiety by this point. She and Mrs. Sharpe edged their way out of the wooden pew from which they had watched an apparently endless procession of accused appear before the bench. A young man who seemed to have been representing most of them approached Mrs. Sharpe.

"Are you Tommy Hatley's mother?" he asked.

"No; that's her there, son."

"Mrs. Hatley," he shook hands with them both, "my name's Oliver McLowry. I'm representing your son."

"Is he all right, Mr. McLowry? What happened to him? When will he be up?"

Mr. McLowry took Margaret gently by the arm and led her and Mrs. Sharpe out of the court and into the now almost deserted foyer.

"Don't be worrying," he told them, "Tommy is in good form. He'll be up about two o'clock this afternoon. I'll see if I can get him bail."

By now the trio—Mr. McLowry in his dark suit between the two middle-aged women in their brighter summer coats—were picking their way down the court steps and into Townhall Street.

"I've to rush back to the office for an appointment, ladies. You'll get a tea or coffee over there in that pub. We'll see how Tommy gets on this afternoon and," he handed Margaret his card, "here's my office number. Phone me tomorrow and my secretary will make an appointment for us to get together to discuss the case. Don't be concerned if Tommy doesn't get bail today. There were a lot of arrests last night and the DPP is opposing bail. Your Tommy has no previous record so he might just be one of the lucky ones."

He smiled again. Margaret scarcely heard what he had been saying.

"When can I see our Tommy?" she asked.

"If he doesn't get bail you'll get a visit after he's up. He's all right, dear. Try not to worry. I must run now."

He shook hands with them both again and hurried off towards Chichester Street. Margaret and Mrs. Sharpe wandered down towards the pub at the corner. They didn't go in: neither of them had been in a pub before. Instead they walked around to the back of the City Hall and had tea and sandwiches in the International Hotel. They barely had their bus fares left when they came out again.

"I'll fix you up, Mrs. Sharpe, later on," Margaret promised. "It's not fair on you spending all that money for such tiny wee sandwiches and not even a crust on them. I'll fix you up as soon as we get home."

"Oh no you won't. You needn't bother your barney fixing me up for nothing. That's what neighbors are for. And anyway, sure didn't I only pay for what I ate myself. Wait till I tell our ones about me and you swanking it in the International."

Margaret chuckled. "Our Tommy'll pay, so he will. It's the least he can do for putting us to all this trouble. He's lucky we let him off so lightly. Let's go back round now and make sure to get our seats."

Tommy was up at two o'clock. He looked pale and disheveled as he stood alone and vulnerable in the dock. He smiled at his mother when Mr. McLowry pleaded his case and he waved at Mrs. Sharpe as the magistrate responded, and then he was led away again.

"What happened?" Margaret asked in disbelief.

"He got remanded for a week," Mrs. Sharpe told her.

"What? A week? What about his bail?" She looked helplessly towards Mr. McLowry, but already he was engrossed in the affairs of another client.

"C'mon," Mrs. Sharpe comforted Margaret, "let's get out of here." She allowed herself to be led from the courtroom.

"We should go home now. The children will be home from school and you're worn out. We can phone Mr. McLowry's office from my house later on," Mrs. Sharpe advised.

"I'm seeing our Tommy, Mrs. Sharpe, so I am, before I go anywhere." They were standing in the foyer. "Mr. McLowry said I could see our Tommy after he was up, so that's what I'm going to do. You go on home and I'll call in on you when I get back. There's no point the two of us waiting here."

"Are you sure?"

"Of course I'm sure, so I am. Your children'll be in. Just do one more wee thing for me. Nip in and tell our Teresa to put on the potatoes if I'm not back in time. And tell her there's money behind the clock if she needs it; tell her to go easy on it, too," she added. "And thank you, Mrs. Sharpe. You're one in a million."

"No problem," Mrs. Sharpe replied. "Tell your Tommy I was asking after him. Tell him I'll bake him an apple cake with a file in it. Cheerio, Margaret. I'm sorry I have to rush off and leave you here."

"Catch yourself on. G'wan out of this with you. I'm going to ask your man the score about seeing our Tommy," Margaret nodded towards a big RUC man standing near by.

"Good luck," said Mrs. Sharpe. "And don't forget to tell Tommy I was asking for him."

"That door down there, missus," the RUC man told Margaret. "The sergeant in there'll have information about prisoners."

Margaret thanked him and made her way to the door marked Enquiries at the end of the foyer. She knocked on it a few times and when there was no reply she pushed it nervously to find herself in front of a counter in a small room. A bald-headed RUC man looked at her with indifference.

"I want to see my son, Tommy Hatley," Margaret informed him. "I was told to come here to see the sergeant."

"Well I'm the sergeant, but whoever told you that doesn't know what he's talking about, missus," he replied coldly.

"My son's a prisoner here. He was just up in Court Three. He's on remand. Mr. McLowry's his solicitor."

Margaret fought down the panic rising in her stomach. The sergeant turned away from her.

"There's no visits with prisoners here, missus."

"I want to see my son, mister," Margaret's voice rose and to her own surprise and the sergeant's annoyance she rapped the counter indignantly with her clenched fist.

"Missus, dear, I've told you: there's no visits for prisoners here."

"I have a right to see my son," Margaret's eyes welled up with tears.

"Missus," the sergeant smiled at her, "you have no fucking rights. Now," the smile switched off, "get out of my office before I arrest you as well."

"I'm not going anywhere," Margaret replied.

"Is that right?" The sergeant's smile returned again.

The sound of the door opening behind Margaret interrupted their verbal duel. It was the RUC man who had sent her to the office. He looked from Margaret to the sergeant.

"All right, Sarge?" he asked. "Your son's up in the Crum', missus," he told Margaret. "C'mon." He shepherded her out of the office.

"Don't mind him," he told her kindly, looking at his watch. "You'll be too late for a visit today but you should get one first thing in the morning."

"He said I've no rights," Margaret told him.

"Well, be that as it may, there's no use us arguing about it," he smiled at her.

"Thanks," Margaret replied. "Thanks for your help."

"No problem, missus."

"By the way," she asked as she walked away from him, "what's the right time?"

"Just after half-two, missus."

That's how Margaret was able to remember more or less exactly when she became a rebel. Or maybe, as she would have put it herself, that was when she started to become a rebel. She doesn't remember a lot about the rest of that day. The house was in bedlam when she got home and although Teresa had done her best the younger ones were complaining and playing up. It was only after her husband got in from work and had his dinner and she told him all her news that she remembered she hadn't had dinner herself. She didn't tell him about the tea and sandwiches in the International Hotel. She was still feeling guilty about that when she went down to Mrs. Sharpe's after the children were safely in bed.

"Margaret, you're wired up," Mrs. Sharpe chided her. "What men don't know'll do them no harm."

The thought was a new one for Margaret. It was also an enjoyable one; it was like when she was a child playing a trick on grownups. She chuckled at Mrs. Sharpe's wisdom.

"Maybe you're right, Mrs. Sharpe."

She went to Belfast Prison at Crumlin Road to see Tommy the following morning. He never got bail. Instead, a month later he received the mandatory six-months sentence for riotous behavior. Margaret's routine changed with this new development; now she had to make time for prison visits. She also missed Tommy's wages. She didn't tell her husband that but he must have known because he gave her a little extra each week.

"For Tommy's parcel," he said, "and maybe he'll want the odd book."

He wanted lots of books. Margaret took to going to Smithfield market each week after her visit to pick through the secondhand bookshops for the novels and political tomes on Tommy's list. She got into the habit also of having tea and a scone in the ITL cafe before heading for home again. That was a new luxury for her as well. She got friendly with one of the booksellers, a woman of her own age called Mary. When Margaret eventually confided to her that the books were for her son in prison, Mary insisted she would send him some as well. She took payment for Margaret's selection only when Margaret threatened not to return if she didn't.

"Here," she laughed, "take this one for yourself."

"Ach, I never get time to read," Margaret protested.

"Make time. Be kind to yourself," Mary said in mock sternness. "You'll get no thanks otherwise."

That's how Margaret started reading, in the ITL cafe over her weekly cup of tea and scone.

That night Teresa and her sisters heard their father's voice raised in exasperation in the bedroom next to them.

"Woman, dear, are you never going to let me get to sleep? I don't know what's come over you!"

They listened intently for a reply. It didn't come for a full minute.

"I just want you to promise not to call me 'mother' again. I'm not your mother. I'm your wife."

"Yes, dear."

"Promise."

"I promise, Margaret, I promise. Anything for peace and quiet."

Teresa smiled to herself. She knew her mother was smiling also. "Good for you, Ma," she whispered.

"What's wrong?" her younger sister asked.

"Nothing," said Teresa proudly. "Our Ma's just become a woman's libber."

Margaret didn't think of herself like that. She had two grownup children married and living away from home; the rest, the youngest of whom was ten, were all living together in a tiny house, they and their father all making demands on her and her time. But she took Mary's advice and Mrs. Sharpe's, and started to make time for herself.

Tommy got out of jail after his six months but was interned a year later in the big swoops. The British Army took his father as well but he was released after a few days. Margaret was up to her neck looking after refugees, taking part in protests: she didn't get to bed for three nights.

When she awoke after fourteen hours solid sleep her husband brought her dinner to her on a tray.

"You never did that before," she smiled in pleased surprise. "Even when I was sick, even when I had our babies. The neighbors or our ones did it."

35

"I'm not the only one who's doing things they never did before," he replied awkwardly. "There's been a queue of people here for you. There's a list of messages. And there's a meeting in St. Paul's, Mrs. Sharpe says."

"What was on the news?" Margaret propped herself up on the pillows and settled the tray on her lap.

"The whole place has gone mad," he replied morosely. "More shooting last night: two killed; more arrests, bombs in the town, people hurt. Will I go on?"

She looked at him quietly. "No, you're okay."

"Where did you get the food?" he asked her, watching as she devoured the sausages and potatoes he'd prepared.

"That's for me to know," she teased him, "and for you to find out. You oul' fellas are all the same; yous need to know everything. Well, for nearly thirty years you've been feeding us and for the last three days I've been feeding us, and I feel good about it."

He looked at her in amazement.

"Ach, love, I'm only joking," she laughed. "You never could take a slagging. I got the food down in St. Paul's. We set up a coordinating committee in the school to look after the refugees and to distribute food, especially baby food and the like. That's what happens when you get arrested, you see. I go mad for the want of you."

She put down her tray and lunged towards him in mock attack. He retreated to the door in embarrassment.

"The whole place has gone mad," he said again. "It's time you were up, woman."

She chuckled at his discomfiture. "I wonder how he gave me all those children," she thought cheerfully.

"My oul' fella never worked," Mrs. Sharpe said to Margaret. "You're lucky. Yours is never idle. I used to say my man put on his working clothes when he was going to bed."

They were sitting together after the meeting.

"It's funny about men," Margaret said, "they are all bound up in wee images of themselves. You know: they're the providers, they take the decisions. They decide everything."

"Or they think they do," Mrs. Sharpe said.

"I know, I know," Margaret agreed, "and as long as we let them think that it's fine and dandy. But as soon as we start to let them see that we can take decisions too and make choices, then their worlds become shaky and their images get tarnished. They, even the best of them, like to keep us in our places."

"Blame their mothers."

"Nawh, that's too simple."

"But it's true."

"I don't know. Young ones nowadays have a better notion of things. I'm no different from my mother but our ones are different from me."

"You're no different from your mother?" Mrs. Sharpe looked at her. "Who're you kidding? Could you see your mother round here doin' what we're doing?"

"No," Margaret replied. "But then she never got the chance: a year ago I couldn't even see myself doing what we're doing."

She got slowly to her feet. "And now I suppose we better get back to our oul' lads. Mine's only started to get used to being married to me. And," she looked at Mrs. Sharpe with a smile in her eyes, "he ain't seen nothing yet."

They laughed together as they locked up the school for the night. Outside, people were gathered at barricades and street corners. They all greeted Margaret and Mrs. Sharpe as they passed. At Mrs. Sharpe's the two women parted and Margaret walked slowly up the street. She was tired, middle-aged and cheerful as she made her way home to liberate her husband.

The Mountains of Mourne

G EORDIE MAYNE LIVED in Urney Street, one of a net-
work of narrow streets which stretched from Cupar Street,
in the shadow of Clonard Monastery, to the Shankill Road.
I don't know where Geordie is now or even if he's living or dead, but
I think of him often. Though I knew him only for a short time many
years ago, Geordie is one of those characters who might come into
your life briefly but never really leave you afterwards.

Urney Street is probably gone now. I haven't been there in
twenty years and all that side of the Shankill has disappeared since
then as part of the redevelopment of the area. Part of the infamous
Peace Line follows the route that Cupar Street used to take. Before
the Peace Line was erected Lawnbrook Avenue joined Cupar Street
to the Shankill Road. Cupar Street used to run from the Falls Road
up until it met Lawnbrook Avenue, then it swung left and ran on
to the Springfield Road. Only as I try to place the old streets do I
realize how much the place has changed this last twenty years, and
how little distance there really is between the Falls and the Shankill.

For all that closeness there might as well be a thousand miles between them.

When we were kids we used to take shortcuts up Cupar Street from the Falls to the Springfield Road. Catholics lived in the bottom end of Cupar Street nearest the Falls; there were one or two in the middle of Cupar Street, too, but the rest were mainly Protestants till you got up past Lawnbrook Avenue and from there to the Springfield Road was all Catholic again. The streets going up the Springfield Road on the righthand side were Protestant and the ones on the left-hand side up as far as the Flush were Catholic. After that both sides were nearly all Protestant until you got to Ballymurphy.

When we were kids we paid no heed to these territorial niceties, though once or twice during the Orange marching season we'd get chased. Around about the Twelfth of July and at other appropriate dates the Orangemen marched through many of those streets, Catholic and Protestant alike. The Catholic ones got special attention, as did individual Catholic houses, with the marching bands and their followers, sometimes the worse for drink, exciting themselves with enthusiastic renderings of Orange tunes as they passed by. The Mackie's workers also passed that way twice daily, an especially large contingent making its way from the Shankill along Cupar Street to Mackie's Foundry. The largest engineering works in the city was surrounded by Catholic streets, but it employed very few Catholics.

Often bemused by expressions such as Catholic street and Protestant area, I find myself nonetheless using the very same expressions. How could a house be Catholic or Protestant? Yet when it comes to writing about the reality it's hard to find other words. Though loath to do so, I use the terms Catholic and Protestant here to encompass the various elements who make up the Unionist and non-Unionist citizens of this state.

It wasn't my intention to tell you all this. I could write a book about the *craic* I had as a child making my way in and out of all those wee streets on the way back and forth to school or the Boys' Confraternity in Clonard or even down at the Springfield Road dam fishing for spricks, but that's not what I set out to tell you about. I set out to tell you about Geordie Mayne of Urney Street. Geordie was an Orangeman, nominally at least. He never talked about it to me except on the occasion when he told me that he was one. His lodge was The Pride of the Shankill Loyal Orange Lodge, I think, though it's hard to be sure after all this time.

I only knew Geordie for a couple of weeks, but even though that may seem too short a time to make a judgment I could never imagine him as a zealot or a bigot. You get so that you can tell, and by my reckoning Geordie wasn't the worst. He was a driver for a big drinks firm: that's how I met him. I was on the run at the time. It was almost Christmas 1969 and I had been running about like a blue-arsed fly since early summer. I hadn't worked since July, we weren't getting any money except a few bob every so often for smokes, so things were pretty rough. But it was an exciting time: I was only twenty-one and I was one of a dozen young men and women who were up to their necks in trying to sort things out.

To say that I was on the run is to exaggerate a little. I wasn't wanted for anything, but I wasn't taking any chances either. I hadn't slept at home since the end of May when the RUC had invaded Hooker Street in Ardoyne and there had been a night or two of sporadic rioting. Most of us who were politically active started to take precautions at that time. We were expecting internment or worse as the civil rights agitation and the reaction against it continued to escalate. Everything came to a head in August, including internment, and in Belfast the conflict had been particularly sharp around Cupar Street. This abated a little, but we thought it was only a temporary respite: with the British Army on the streets it couldn't be long till things hotted up again. In the meantime we were not making ourselves too available.

Conway Street, Cupar Street at the Falls Road end and all of Norfolk Street had been completely burned out on the first night of the August pogrom; further up, near the monastery, Bombay Street was gutted on the following night. These were all Catholic streets. Urney Street was just a stone's throw from Bombay Street; that is, if you were a stone thrower.

The drinks company Geordie worked for was taking on extra help to cope with the Christmas rush, and a few of us went up to the head office on the Glen Road on spec one morning; as luck would have it I got a start, together with Big Eamonn and two others. I was told to report to the store down in Cullingtree Road the next morning and it was there that I met Geordie.

He saw me before I saw him. I was standing in the big yard among all the vans and lorries and I heard this voice shouting: "Joe...Joe Moody."

I paid no attention.

"Hi, boy! Is your name Joe Moody?" the voice repeated.

With a start I realized that that was indeed my name, or at least it was the bum name I'd given when I'd applied for the job.

"Sorry," I stammered.

"I thought you were corned beef. C'mon over here."

I did as instructed and found myself beside a well-built, red-haired man in his late thirties. He was standing at the back of a large empty van.

"Let's go, our kid. My name's Geordie Mayne. We'll be working together. We're late. Have you clocked in? Do it over there and then let's get this thing loaded up."

He handed me a sheaf of dockets.

"Pack them in that order. Start from the back. I'll only be a minute."

He disappeared into the back of the store. I had hardly started to load the van when he arrived back. Between the two of us we weren't long packing in the cartons and crates of wines and spirits and then we were off, Geordie cheerfully saluting the men on barricade duty at the end of the street as they waved us out of the Falls area and into the rest of the world.

Geordie and I spent most of our first day together delivering our load to off-licenses and public houses in the city center. I was nervous of being recognized because I had worked in a bar there but luckily it got its deliveries from a different firm. It was the first day I had been in the city center since August; except for the one trip to

Dublin and one up to Derry I had spent all my time behind the barricades. It was disconcerting to find that, apart from the unusual sight of British soldiers with their cheerful, arrogant voices, life in the center of Belfast, or at least its licensed premises, appeared unaffected by the upheavals of the past few months. It was also strange as we made our deliveries to catch glimpses on television of news coverage about the very areas and issues I was so involved in and familiar with. Looked at from outside through the television screen, the familiar scenes might as well have been in another country.

Geordie and I said nothing of any of this to one another. That was a strange experience for me, too. My life had been so full of the cut-and-thrust of analysis, argument and counter-argument about everything that affected the political situation that I found it difficult to restrain myself from commenting on events to this stranger. Indeed, emerging from the close camaraderie of my closed world, as I had done only that morning, I found it unusual even to be with a stranger. Over a lunch of soup and bread rolls in the Harp Bar in High Street I listened to the midday news on the BBC's Radio Ulster while all the time pretending indifference. The lead item was a story about an IRA convention and media speculation about a republican split. It would be nightfall before I would be able to check this out for myself, though a few times during the day I almost left Geordie in his world of cheerful pubs and publicans for the security of the ghettos.

The next few days followed a similar pattern. Each morning started with Geordie absenting himself for a few minutes to the back of the store while I started loading up the van. Then we were off from within the no-go areas and into the city center. By the end of the first week the two of us were like old friends. Our avoidance of political topics, even of the most pressing nature, that unspoken and much-used form of political protection and survival developed through expediency, had in its own way been a political indicator, a signal, that we came from "different sides."

In the middle of the second week Geordie broke our mutual and instinctive silence on this issue when with a laugh he handed me that morning's dockets. "Well, our kid, this is your lucky day. You're going to see how the other half lives. We're for the Shankill."

My obvious alarm fueled his amusement.

"Oh, aye," he guffawed. "It's all right for me to traipse up and down the Falls every day but my wee Fenian friend doesn't want to return the favor."

I was going to tell him that nobody from the Falls went up the Shankill burning down houses but I didn't. I didn't want to hurt his feelings, but I didn't want to go up the Shankill either. I was in a quandary and set about loading up our deliveries with a heavy heart. After I had only two of the cartons loaded I went to the back of the store to tell Geordie that I was jacking it in. He was in the wee office with oul' Harry the storeman. Each of them had a glass of spirits in his hand. Geordie saw me coming and offered his to me.

"Here, our kid, it's best Jamaicay rum. A bit of Dutch courage never did anyone any harm."

"Nawh thanks, Geordie, I don't drink spirits. I need to talk to you for a minute. . . "

"If it's about today's deliveries, you've nothing to worry about. We've only one delivery up the Shankill and don't be thinking of not going 'cos you'll end up out on your arse. It's company policy that mixed crews deliver all over the town. Isn't that right, Harry?"

Harry nodded in agreement.

"C'mon, our kid. I'll do the delivery for you. Okay? You can sit in the van. How's that grab you? Can't be fairer than that, can I, Harry?"

"Nope," Harry grunted. They drained their glasses.

"I'll take a few beers for the child, Harry," Geordie said over his shoulder as he and I walked back to the van.

"You know where they are," said Harry.

"Let's go," said Geordie to me. "It's not every day a wee Fenian like you gets on to the best road in Belfast. . ." he grabbed me around the neck ". . . and off it again in one piece. Hahaha."

That's how I ended up on the Shankill. It wasn't so bad but before I tell you about that, in case I forget, from then on, each morning when Geordie returned from the back of the store after getting his "wee drop of starting fuel" he always had a few bottles of beer for me.

Anyway, back to the job in hand. As Geordie said, we only had the one order on the Shankill. It was to the Long Bar. We drove up by Unity Flats and on to Peter's Hill. There were no signs of barricades like the ones on the Falls, and apart from a patrolling RUC Landrover and two British Army Jeeps the road was the same as it had always seemed to me. Busy and prosperous and coming awake in the early winter morning sunshine.

A few months earlier, in October, the place had erupted in protest at the news that the B-Specials were to be disbanded. The protesters had killed one RUC man and wounded three others; thirteen British soldiers had been injured. In a night of heavy gunfighting along the Shankill Road the British had killed two civilians and wounded twenty others. Since then there had been frequent protests here against the existence of no-go areas in Catholic parts of Belfast and Derry.

Mindful of all this, I perched uneasily in the front of the van, ready at a second's notice to spring into Geordie's seat and drive like the blazes back whence I came. I needn't have worried. Geordie was back in moments. As he climbed into the driver's seat he threw me a packet of cigarettes.

"There's your Christmas box, our kid. I told them I had a wee Fenian out here and that you were dying for a smoke."

Then he took me completely by surprise.

"Do y' fancy a fish supper? It's all right! We eat fish on Friday as well. Hold on!"

And before I could say anything he had left me again as he sprinted from the van into the Eagle Supper Saloon.

"I never got any breakfast," he explained on his return. "We'll go 'round to my house. There's nobody in."

I said nothing as we turned into Westmoreland Street and in through a myriad of backstreets till we arrived in Urney Street. Here the tension was palpable, for me at least. Geordie's house was no different from ours. A two bedroomed house with a toilet in the backyard and a modernized scullery. Only for the picture of the British Queen, I could have been in my own street. I buttered rounds of plain white bread and we wolfed down our fish suppers with lashings of Geordie's tea.

Afterwards, my confidence restored slightly, while Geordie was turning the van in the narrow street I walked down to the corner and gazed along the desolation of Cupar Street up towards what remained of Bombay Street. A British soldier in a sandbagged emplacement greeted me in a John Lennon accent.

"'Lo, moite. How's about you?"

I ignored him and stood momentarily immersed in the bleak pitifulness of it all, from the charred remains of the small houses to where the world-weary slopes of Divis Mountain gazed benignly in their winter greenness down on us where we slunk, blighted, below the wise steeples of Clonard. It was Geordie's impatient honking of the horn that shook me out of my reverie. I nodded to the British soldier as I departed. This time he ignored me.

"Not a pretty sight," Geordie said as I climbed into the van beside him.

I said nothing. We made our way back through the side-streets on to the Shankill again in silence. As we turned into Royal Avenue at the corner of North Street he turned to me.

"By the way," he said, "I wasn't there that night."

There was just a hint of an edge in his voice.

"I'm sorry! I'm not blaming you," I replied. "It's not your fault."

"I know," he told me firmly.

That weekend, subsidized by my week's wages, I was immersed once more in subversion. That at least was how the Unionist government viewed the flurry of political activity in the ghettos and indeed a similar view was taken by those representatives of the Catholic middle class who had belatedly attached themselves to the various committees in which some of us had long been active. On Monday I was back delivering drink.

We spent the week before Christmas in County Down, seemingly a million miles from the troubles and the tension of Belfast town. For the first time in years I did no political work. It was late by the time we got back each night and I was too tired, so that by Wednesday I realized that I hadn't even seen, read or heard any news all that week. I smiled to myself at the thought that both I and the struggle appeared to be surviving without each other; in those days that was a big admission for me to make, even to myself.

In its place Geordie and I spent the week up and down country roads, driving through beautiful landscapes, over and around hilltops and along rugged seashores and loughsides as we ferried our liquid wares from village to town, from town to port and back to village again; from market town to fishing village, from remote hamlet to busy crossroads. Even yet the names have a magical sound for me and at each one Geordie and I took the time for a stroll or a quick look at some local antiquity.

One memorable day we journeyed out to Comber and from there to Killyleagh and Downpatrick, to Crossgar and back again and along the Ballyhornan road and on out to Strangford where we ate our cooked ham baps and drank bottles of stout, hunkering down from the wind below the square tower of Strangford Castle, half-frozen with the cold as we looked over towards Portaferry on the opposite side, at the edge of the Ards Peninsula. We spent a day there as well, and by this time I had a guide book with me written by Richard Hayward, and I kept up a commentary as we toured the peninsula, from Millisle the whole way around the coastline and back to Newtownards. By the end of the week we had both seen where the Norsemen had settled and the spot where Thomas Russell, "the man from God knows where," was hanged, where Saint Patrick had lived and Cromwell and Betsy Grey and Shane O'Neill. We visited monastic settlements and stone circles, round towers, dolmens and holy wells. Up and down the basket-of-eggs county we walked old battle-sites like those of the faction fights at Dolly's Brae or Scarva, "wee buns" we learned compared to Saintfield where Munroe and 7,000 United Irishmen routed the English forces, or the unsuccessful three-year siege by the Great O'Neill, the Earl of Tyrone, of Jordan's Castle at Ardglass. And in between all this we delivered our cargoes of spirits and fine wines.

This was a new world to me, and to Geordie too. It was a marked contrast to the smoke and smell and claustrophobic closeness of our Belfast ghettos and the conflicting moods which gripped them in that winter of 1969. Here was the excitement of greenery and wildlife, of rushing water, of a lightness and heady clearness in the atmosphere and of strange magic around ancient pagan holy places. We planned our last few days' runs as tours and loaded the van accordingly so that whereas in the city we took the shortest route, now we steered according to Richard Hayward's guide book.

On Christmas Eve we went first to Newry where we unloaded over half our supplies in a series of drops at that town's licensed premises. By lunchtime we were ready for the run along the coast road to Newcastle, skirting the Mournes, and from there back home. At our last call on the way out to the Warrenpoint Road, the publican set us up two pints as a Christmas box. The pub was empty and as we sat there enjoying the sup a white-haired man in his late sixties came in. He was out of breath, weighed down with a box full of groceries.

"A bully, John," he greeted the publican. "Have I missed the bus?"

"Indeed and you have, Paddy, and he waited for you for as long as he could."

Paddy put his box down on the floor. His face was flushed.

"Well, God's curse on it anyway. I met Peadar Hartley and big MacCaughley up the town and the pair of them on the tear and nothing would do them boys but we'd have a Christmas drink and then another till they put me off my whole way of going with their ceiling and oul' palavering. And now I've missed the bloody bus. God's curse on them two rogues. It'll be dark before there's another one."

He sighed resignedly and pulled a stool over to the bar, saluting the two of us as he did so.

"John, I might as well have a drink when I'm this far and give these two men one as well."

He overruled our protests.

"For the season that's in it. One more'll do yous no harm. It's Christmas. Isn't that right, John? And one for yourself and I'll have a wee Black Bush meself."

"Will you have anything in the Bush, Paddy?"

"Indeed and I'll not. Now John, if it was Scotch now I'd have to have water or ginger ale or something but that's only with Scotch. I take nothing in my whiskey!"

We all joined him in his delighted laughter.

"What way are yous going, boys? Did you say yous were going out towards Newcastle?" the publican asked us.

Geordie nodded.

"Could you ever drop oul' Paddy out that road? He has to go as far as Kilkeel and by the looks of him if he doesn't go soon he'll be here till the New Year."

"No problem," Geordie grinned. I could see he was enjoying the old man who was now lilting merrily away to himself.

"De euw did eh euw, did eh euw did del de."

"Paddy, these two men'll give you a wee lift home."

Paddy was delighted.

"Surely to God, boys, but yous is great men so yous are. Here, we'll have another wee one before we go. A wee *deoch don dorais*.* All right, John?"

"Indeed and it isn't," John told him. "Kate'll be worrying about you and these two lads can't wait. Isn't that right, boys?"

"Well, let it never be said that I kept men from their work," Paddy compromised.

"A happy New Year to you, John." The three of us saluted our host and retreated into the crisp afternoon air.

"It'll snow the night," our newfound friend and passenger announced, sniffing the air. I was carrying his box.

He did a jig, to Geordie's great amusement, when he saw that we were travelling in a drinks van.

"It'll be the talk of the place!" he laughed as we settled him into the passenger seat while I wedged myself against the door. Geordie gave him a bottle of stout as we pulled away.

"Do you want a glass?" I asked. "There's some here."

---

* One for the road

"A glass? Sure yous are well organized. Yous must be from Belfast! No, son, I don't need a glass, thanks all the same. This is grand by the neck. By the way, my name's Paddy O'Brien."

We introduced ourselves.

"You'll never get a job in the shipyard with a name like that," Geordie slagged him.

"And I wouldn't want it. 'Tis an Orange hole, begging your pardon lads and no offense, but them that's there neither works nor wants."

To my relief Geordie guffawed loudly, winking at me as he did. For the rest of the journey Paddy regaled us with stories of his mishaps in black holes and other places.

"I wouldn't like to live in Belfast. I'll tell yous that for sure. I worked there often enough, in both quarters mind you, and I always found the people as decent as people anywhere else. I was at the building and I went often enough to Casement Park, surely to God I did, for the football and some grand games I saw, but I wouldn't live there. Thon's a tough town!"

"It's not so bad," I said loyally, while all the time looking beyond Paddy and past Geordie to where Narrow Water flashed past us and the hills of County Louth dipped their toes in Carlingford Bay.

"No, give me the Mournes," Paddy persisted. "Were yous ever in the Mournes?" He emphasized "in."

"Nawh," we told him. Geordie began to enthuse about our week journeying around the county.

"Sure yous have a great time of it," Paddy agreed. "I'll come with yous the next time. Work? Yous wouldn't know what work was. But boys, I'm telling yous this. Don't be leaving this day without going into the Mournes. There's a road yous could take, wouldn't be out of your way, so it wouldn't. After yous drop me off, go on towards Annalong on this road, and a wee bit outside the village on the Newcastle side there's a side road at Glassdrummond that'll take you up to Silent Valley. It's a straight road from here right through to Glassdrummond, boys. Yous can't miss it."

"That sounds good to me," Geordie agreed.

"Well, that's the best I can do for yous, boys. Come back some day and I'll take yous on better roads right into the heart of the mountains, but it'll be dark soon and snowing as well and my Kate'll kill me, so the Silent Valley'll have t' do yous. You'll be able to see where yous Belfast ones gets your good County Down water from to water your whiskey with and to wash your necks."

"Is Slieve Donard the highest of the Mournes?" I asked, trying to find my faithful guide book below Paddy's seat.

"Donard? The highest? It'll only take you a couple of hours to climb up there; but, boys, you could see the whole world from Slieve Donard. That's where Saint Donard had his cell, up on the summit. You'll see the Isle of Man out to the east and up along our own coast all of Strangford Lough and up to the hills of Belfast and the smoke rising above them, and beyond that on a clear day Lough Neagh and as far as Slieve Gallion on the Derry and Tyrone border. And southwards beyond Newry you'll see Slieve Gullion, where Cúchulainn rambled, and Slieve Foy east of there, behind Carlingford town, and farther south again you'll see the Hill of Howth and beyond that again if the day is good the Sugar Loaf and the Wicklow Mountains'll just be on the horizon."

"That's some view," Geordie said in disbelief.

Paddy hardly heard as he looked pensively ahead at the open road.

"There's only one thing you can't see from Donard, and many people can't see it anyway although it's the talk of the whole place, and even if it jumped up and bit you it's not to be seen from up there among all the sights. Do yous know what I'm getting at, boys? It's the cause of all our cursed troubles, and if you were twice as high as Donard you couldn't see it. Do yous know what it is?"

We both waited expectantly, I with a little trepidation, for him to enlighten us.

"The bloody border," he announced eventually. "You can't see that awful bloody imaginary line that they pretend can divide the air and the mountain ranges and the rivers, and all it really divides is the people. You can see everything from Donard, but isn't it funny you can't see that bloody border?"

I could see Geordie's hands tighten slightly on the steering-wheel. He continued smiling all the same.

"And there's something else," Paddy continued. "Listen to all the names: Slieve Donard, or Bearnagh or Meelbeg or Meelmore—all in our own language. For all their efforts they've never killed that either. Even most of the wee Orange holes: what are they called? Irish names. From Ballymena to Ahoghill to the Shankill, Aughrim, Derry and the Boyne. The next time yous boys get talking to some of them Belfast Orangemen you should tell them that."

"I'm a Belfast Orangeman," Geordie told him before I could say a word. I nearly died, but Paddy laughed uproariously. I said nothing. I could see that Geordie was starting to take the needle. We passed through Kilkeel with only Paddy's chortling breaking the silence.

"You're the quare *craic*," he laughed. "I've really enjoyed this wee trip. Yous are two decent men. *Tá mise go han buíoch daoibh, a cháirde.* I'm very grateful to you indeed."

"*Tá fáilte romhat*," I said, glad in a way that we were near his journey's end.

"Oh, *maith an fear*," he replied. "*Tabhair dom do lámh.*" We shook hands.

"What d'fuck's yous two on about?" Geordie interrupted angrily.

"He's only thanking us and I'm telling him he's welcome," I explained quickly. "Shake hands with him!"

Geordie did so grudgingly as the old man directed him to stop by the side of the road.

"Happy Christmas," he proclaimed as he lifted his box.

"Happy Christmas," we told him. He stretched across me and shook hands with Geordie again.

"*Go n'éirigh an bóthar libh*," he said. "May the road rise before you."

"And you," I shouted, pulling closed the van door as Geordie drove off quickly and Paddy and his box vanished into the shadows.

"Why don't yous talk bloody English," Geordie snarled savagely at me as he slammed through the gears and catapulted the van forward.

"He just wished you a safe journey," I said lamely. "He had too much to drink and he was only an old man. It is Christmas after all."

"That's right, you stick up for him. He wasn't slow about getting his wee digs in, Christmas or no Christmas. I need a real drink after all that oul' balls."

He pulled the van roughly into the verge again. I got out too as he clambered outside and climbed into the back. Angrily he selected a carton of whiskey from among its fellows and handed me a yellow bucket which was wedged in among the boxes.

"Here, hold this," he ordered gruffly. As I did so he held the whiskey box at arm's length above his head and then, to my surprise, dropped it on the road. We heard glass smashing and splintering as the carton crumpled at one corner. Geordie pulled the bucket from me and sat the corner of the whiskey box into it.

"Breakages," he grinned at my uneasiness. "You can't avoid them. By the time we get to Paddy's Silent bloody Valley there'll be a nice wee drink for us to toast him and the border *and* that bloody foreign language of yours. Take that in the front with you."

I did as he directed. Already the whiskey was beginning to drip into the bucket.

"That's an old trick," Geordie explained as we continued our journey. He was still in bad humor and maybe even a little embarrassed about the whiskey, which continued to dribble into the bucket between my feet on the floor. "The cardboard acts as a filter and stops any glass from getting through. Anyway, it's Christmas and Paddy isn't the only one who can enjoy himself," he concluded as we took the side road at Glassdrummond and commenced the climb up to the Silent Valley.

The view that awaited us was indeed breathtaking, as we came suddenly upon the deep mountain valley with its massive dam and huge expanse of water surrounded by rugged mountains and skirted by a picturesque stretch of road.

"Well, Paddy was right about this bit anyway," Geordie conceded as he parked the van and we got out for a better view. "It's a pity we didn't take a camera with us," he said. "It's gorgeous here. Give's the bucket and two of them glasses."

52

He filled the two glasses and handed me one.

"Don't mind me, our kid. I'm not at myself. Here's to a good Christmas."

That was the first time I drank whiskey. I didn't want to offend Geordie again by refusing but I might as well have for I put my foot in it anyway the next minute. He was gazing reflectively up the valley, quaffing his drink with relish while I sipped timorously on mine.

"Do you not think you're drinking too much to be driving?" I asked.

He exploded.

"Look son, I've stuck you for a few weeks now, and I never told you once how to conduct your affairs; not once. You've gabbled on at me all week about every bloody thing under the sun and today to make matters worst you and that oul' degenerate that I was stupid enough to give a lift to, you and him tried to coerce me and talked about me in your stupid language, and now you're complaining about my drinking. When you started as my helper I didn't think I'd have to take the pledge *and* join the fuckin' rebels as well. Give my head peace, would you wee lad; for the love and honor of God, give's a bloody break!"

His angry voice skimmed across the water and bounced back at us off the side of the mountains. I could feel the blood rushing to my own head as the whiskey and Geordie's words registered in my brain.

"Who the hell do you think you are, eh?" I shouted at him, and my voice clashed with the echo of his as they collided across the still waters.

"Who do I think I am? Who do you think you are is more like it," he snapped back, "with all your bright ideas about history and language and all that crap. You and that oul' eejit Paddy are pups from the same Fenian litter, but you remember one thing, young fella-me-lad, yous may have the music and songs and history and even the bloody mountains, but we've got everything else; you remember that!"

His outburst caught me by surprise.

"All that is yours as well, Geordie. We don't keep it from you. It's you that rejects it all. It doesn't reject you. It's not ours to give or take. You were born here same as me."

"I don't need you to tell me what's mine. I know what's mine. I know where I was born. You can keep all your emotional crap. Like I said, we've got all the rest."

"Who's we, Geordie? Eh? Who's we? The bloody English Queen or Lord bloody Terence O'Neill, or Chi Chi, the dodo that's in charge now? Is that who we is? You've got all the rest! Is that right, Geordie? That's shit and you know it."

I grabbed him by the arm and spun him round to face me. For a minute I thought he was going to hit me. I was ready for him. But he said nothing as we stood glaring at each other.

"You've got fuck all, Geordie," I told him. "Fuck all except a two-bedroomed house in Urney Street and an identity crisis."

He turned away from me and hurled his glass into the darkening distance.

"This'll nivver be Silent Valley again, not after we're finished with it," he laughed heavily. "I'm an Orangeman, Joe. That's what I am. It's what my Da was. I don't agree with everything here. My Da wouldn't even talk to a Papist, nivver mind drink or work with one. When I was listening to Paddy I could see why. That's what all this civil rights rubbish is about as well. Well, I don't mind people having their civil rights. That's fair enough. But you know and I know if it wasn't that it would be something else. I'm easy come, easy go. There'd be no trouble if everybody else was the same."

I had quietened down also by now.

"But people need their rights," I said.

"Amn't I only after saying that!" he challenged me.

"Well, what are you going to do about it?" I retorted.

"Me?" he laughed. "Now I know your head's cut! I'm going to do exactly nothing about it! There are a few things that make me different from you. We've a lot in common, I grant you that, but we're different also, and one of the differences is that after Christmas I'll have a job and you won't, and I intend to keep it. And more importantly, I intend to stay alive to do it."

"Well, that's straight enough and there's no answer to that," I mused, sipping the last of my whiskey.

Geordie laughed at me.

"Typical Fenian," he commented. "I notice you didn't throw away your drink."

"What we have we hold." I took another wee sip and gave him the last of it.

"By the way, seeing we're talking to each other instead of at each other, there's no way that our ones, and that includes me, will ever let Dublin rule us."

The sun was setting and there was a few wee flurries of snow in the air.

"Why not?" I asked.

"'Cos that's the way it is."

"What we have we hold?" I repeated. "Only for real."

"If you like."

"But you've nothing in common with the English. We don't need them here to rule us. We can do a better job ourselves. They don't care about the Unionists. You go there and they treat you like a Paddy just like me. What do you do with all your loyalty then? You're Irish. Why not claim that and we'll all govern Dublin."

"I'm British!"

"So am I," I exclaimed. "Under duress 'cos I was born in this state. We're both British subjects but we're Irishmen. Who do you support in the rugby? Ireland I bet! Or international soccer? The same! All your instincts and roots and . . ." I waved my arms around at the dusky mountains in frustration ". . . surroundings are Irish. This is fucking Ireland. It's County Down, not Sussex or Suffolk or Yorkshire. It's us and we're it!" I shouted.

"Now you're getting excited again. You shouldn't drink whiskey," Geordie teased me. "It's time we were going. C'mon; I surrender."

On the way down to Newcastle I drank the whiskey that was left in the bucket. We had only one call to make, so when I asked him to, Geordie dropped me at the beach. I stood watching as the van drove off and thought that perhaps he wouldn't return for me. It was dark by now. As I walked along the strand the snow started in earnest. Slieve Donard was but a hulking shadow behind me. I couldn't see it. Here I was in Newcastle, on the beach. On my own, in the dark. Drunk. On Christmas Eve. Waiting for a bloody Orangeman to come back for me so that I could go home.

The snow was lying momentarily on the sand, and the water rushing in to meet it looked strange in the moonlight as it and the sand and the snow merged. I was suddenly exhilarated by my involvement with all these elements and as I crunched the sand and snow beneath my feet and the flakes swirled around me my earlier frustrations disappeared. Then I chuckled aloud at the irony of it all.

The headlights of the van caught me in their glare. My Orangeman had returned.

"You're soaked, you bloody eejit," he complained when I climbed into the van again.

He, too, was in better form. As we drove home it was as if we had never had a row. We had a sing-song—mostly carols with some Beatles numbers—and the both of us stayed well clear of any contentious verses. On the way through the Belfast suburbs Geordie sang what we called "our song."

> O Mary, this London's a wonderful sight
> There's people here working by day and by night:
> They don't grow potatoes or barley or wheat,
> But there's gangs of them digging for gold in the street.
> At least when I asked them that's what I was told,
> So I took a hand at this digging for gold,
> For all that I found there I might as well be
> Where the Mountains of Mourne sweep down to the sea.

We went in for a last drink after we'd clocked out at the store, but by this time my head was thumping and I just wanted to go home.

As we walked back to the van Geordie shook my hand warmly.

"Thanks, kid. I've learned a lot this last week or so, and not just about County Down. You're dead on, son," he smiled, "for a Fenian. Good luck to you anyway, oul' hand, in all that you do, but just remember, our kid, I love this place as much as you do."

"I know," I said. "I learned that much at least."

He dropped me off at Divis Street and drove off waving, on across the Falls towards the Shankill. I walked up to the Falls. That was the last I saw of Geordie Mayne. I hope he has survived the last twenty years and that he'll survive the next twenty as well. I hope we'll meet again in better times. He wasn't such a bad fella, for an Orangeman.

Up the Rebels

SEAMUS HAD BECOME institutionalized. He had been serving terms of twelve months, or six months, or three months in Belfast Prison for as long as he or anyone else could remember. It had gone on for so long now that he had forgotten how to cope with even the simplest realities of life outside. Three meals a day, a bed in a cell and the absence of decision-making on any issue, from going to the toilet to what to eat, had made Seamus into a passive, if likeable, human zombie.

Every time he finished one sentence, back he came again within a week or so, to do time for some equally trivial offense. His family, who were both well-to-do and well-respected, were embarrassed by his behavior. Once they even sent him from the family home in Armagh to Belfast for examination by a psychiatrist. Seamus, for his part, was so disturbed by this experience that he stole the psychiatrist's car and promptly ended back in the relative safety of Belfast Prison again.

That's when I met him. I was on remand at the time he returned to his old job as orderly in A Wing. He used to "bump out" the wing three times a day, and when I was on my way from my cell on the bottom landing or sitting in it during lock-up I used to see or hear Seamus "bumping" his way up and down the well-polished floor. "Bumping" meant polishing the tiles which stretched a hundred yards from the "circle" up to the end of the wing, and Seamus had been doing it for so long that he now took a certain pride in the dull red glow which was produced by his endless to-ing and fro-ing. He used a bumper, which is like a brush but bigger, with a wooden box where the brush-head should be. The box was weighted down with bricks and its base covered with blankets. It was heavy and tedious work pushing and pulling this contraption over the tiles, all the time trying to coax a shine from them. Seamus didn't seem to mind. The screws didn't really bother him except when they wanted their tea made or some menial task performed. When they did require his services he complied with a slow yet unhesitating obedience. Sometimes one or two of the nastier ones would poke fun at him but he was so much a part of the place that everyone usually took him for granted.

On Sundays, during mass in the prison chapel when the political and the ordinary prisoners came together, we would pass him ciga rettes and at night when we were locked up and he was still bumping up and down the silent, deserted wing we would slip newspapers under our cell doors for him.

He was always extremely cautious about associating too openly with us. We were fairly rebellious, holding parades in the prison yard, segregating ourselves from loyalist prisoners and dealing with the prison administration only through our elected OC. We were continuously on punishment, being subjected to loss of privileges and petty restrictions.

As he bumped back and forth, Seamus was a silent, indifferent observer of the daily battles between us and the screws. Or so, at least, it appeared to us. Then one day a screw spilled a bucket of dirty water over Seamus's clean floor.

"If you don't keep this place cleaner than that," the screw guldered, "I'll have you moved to the base."

Seamus looked at him in dumb disbelief and then, with tears trickling slowly down his face, he went on his hands and knees at the screw's feet to mop up the water which was spreading like a grey blemish over his floor. The screw was a new one, and that incident was only the first of many. It got so bad subsequently that poor Seamus was even afraid to accept our cigarettes and we found the newspapers which we slipped into the hall for him still lying there when we slopped out the following morning.

There wasn't much we could do about it. We willed Seamus to resist and our OC went as far as to make a complaint about the screw, whom we all spontaneously ostracized. But we were beginning also to despise Seamus for showing no signs of fighting back, and in his own way he seemed to be blaming us for his troubles.

And then Seamus rebelled. I was coming from the toilet at the time. He stood only a few yards from me, bumper at hand, looking at a group of screws loitering outside the dining-hall.

"Fuck yous!" he screamed, his words echoing along the wing and up along the tiers of the high glass ceiling.

"Fuck yous!" he screamed again. "Yous think yous are somebody ordering me about. And you," he rounded on me with a vengeance. "Fuck you too and your cigarettes and your stupid bloody newspapers. I'm sick of yous all and your awful bloody floor."

At that the wing exploded into noise, with prisoners banging their cell doors, rattling the bars and generally making a hectic, frantic and frightening clamor.

"Tell them to bangle their floor, Seamus."

"C'mon Seamus, let it all out."

The screws, caught unaware by the suddenness and the ferocity of the din, moved hesitantly out of the wing and into the circle. There, safe behind the heavily barred gates, they looked up towards where Seamus and I stood, unescorted and alone, in the middle of the wing. The closed cell doors stared blankly at us, the floor stretched sullenly to meet the prison walls and the noise continued unabated from all sides. Down at the circle the screws had drawn their batons, and one of them was phoning for assistance.

"Shit," said Seamus to me, a slow, sheepish grin creeping across his face as he surveyed the scene and heard the shouts of encouragement ringing out from all quarters.

"Ah, c'mon," I said, glancing nervously at the circle where reinforcements had begun to arrive. "We better go down there and let them quare fellas know there's nothing wrong." I had to shout to be heard above the continuing noise. "If this keeps up they'll think it's a break-out and you and me'll be murdered."

Seamus ignored me and sat back on his bumper. He took a crumpled roll-up from behind his ear and lit it, slowly and defiantly exhaling the smoke towards the circle.

"I've only a week to do anyway," he muttered. "Sit down and take it easy. We'll go when I'm ready."

And so we did, he to the punishment block and me back to my cell.

He didn't appear back on the wing for a few days after that but the screws told us that he was okay and for what that was worth we were content enough. A new orderly came to bump the wing and life returned to its monotonous normality. Then, on a Thursday, Seamus returned: we greeted him with a shouted, uproarious welcome. The screws didn't seem to mind. He was due for release anyway the following day and there was little they could do about it.

That night, after lock-up, a muffled knock brought me to the cell door. I peered through the narrow chink between the heavy door and the door-frame.

"Do you want a cup of tea?" Seamus hissed in at me. "Hurry up if you do."

I grabbed my mug, delighted at the thought of such an unexpected luxury, and hissed back at him: "How're you going to get the tea in here?"

"Shut up," he ordered. "Houl' your mug up to the chink."

I did as I was told and smiled to myself as the end of a folded newspaper appeared through the narrow gap.

"Widen out the end of the paper and houl' your mug below it."

As I did so a trickle of strong, hot tea poured down the funnel-like folds of the newspaper into my waiting mug.

"Enjoy that," said Seamus. "There's no bromide in it." He withdrew his tea-sodden paper.

"I've more for some of the other lads but I'll have to hurry up before the screws come back." He hesitated for a second: "I'm sorry for giving off the other day. You know the score yourself: I was doing heavy whack. Anyway, I won't be back here again," he added with feeling, "so good luck."

"Good luck, Seamus," I whispered.

He moved from the door, then turned back again. Through the chink I could see his lips widen into a grin.

"Up the rebels," he smiled.

That was the last I saw of him. I was released myself a few months later and I forgot about Seamus. That is, until this morning, when his photograph stared out at me from the front page of the *Irish News*.

Twenty-nine-year-old Co. Armagh man shot dead after crashing through a British Army road-block in a stolen car.

At least he never did go back there again, I thought to myself. But you never know. Maybe he was on his way back when he was killed? Probably not though. Whatever institutionalized refuge Belfast Prison held for him had been lost during his last stay there. They'd never let him bump out A Wing floor again after his last outburst. We'd made sure of that.

No, he probably knew what he was doing when he crashed that road-block.

What was it he had said to me that night he gave me the tea? Up the rebels?

"Aye, Seamus, up the rebels."

Shane

OUR SHANE COST £10. In 1968 £10 was a tidy bit of money. I bought him off Billy Bradley in Springhill. Billy bred Alsatians; he called them German Shepherds. Shane was the only sable-colored pup in a large litter of black-and-tans in Billy's coalshed.

He was a big pup, heavy-boned and thick-coated. I paid for him in two installments. To tell the truth, I have a vague recollection that our Paddy may have paid £5. At least I remember us having an argument, half-joking, half-serious, about who owned what half of the dog, so I suppose that means our Paddy must have been a half-owner. I must ask him about that the next time I see him.

A few weeks after I got Shane, Billy give me his papers. I was pleased about that at first but later I must confess I got a wee bit skeptical. That was after Barney McLavery scoffed when I showed him the papers one day. Barney had remarked on how fine-looking a pup Shane was. Barney bred greyhounds.

"He's champion stock," I said proudly, "pedigree breeding. I've the papers."

"Aye," said Barney, "I wouldn't pay much heed to papers. Doggy-men always have papers about the place. But he's a nice pup all the same."

After that I put the papers away.

We always had a dog in the house. In fact, when I got our Shane we already had a red-haired collie-type mongrel called Mickey I got for nothing from a man in Moyard. Before Mickey we had Rory. I remember when Rory disappeared that I cried for a week. Rory and me and my friends used to roam the Black and Divis mountains every summer. He was a great dog. So was Mickey, and he and Shane made a nice pair. I suppose it's a good thing rearing a young dog with an older dog. The older dog puts manners on the pup.

Then when he was about nine months old Shane got sick. I took him down to the free vet in May Street. Shane had distemper. The vet gave him an injection and told me if he didn't improve that I'd have to get him put down. I was shattered. I took him home on the bus and my Da let me keep him in the back hall. He was very, very sick. I gave him penicillin tablets, force-fed him honey to bring the phlegm up, and washed the mucus from his nose.

"Make him eat," Billy Bradley advised me. "Keep his strength up."

I sat up all night for a week spoon-feeding Shane with scrambled eggs, milk, rusks and water. When he got better I was really proud of myself. Even now, thinking back on it, I'm still proud of myself. And of Shane too, of course. He was banjaxed; anybody would be. But after a few weeks you'd never think he'd had anything wrong with him. Except when he was tired, like after a long walk: then you'd see his back legs a bit weak. Other than that he was all right.

He and I used to go everywhere together until, as things became more hectic, I started spending less time at home. Even then, though, I would still see him regularly and we would walk together maybe three or four times a week. I've always thought there is nothing as relaxing as strolling with a dog. Shane was a really fine-looking animal, and bid-dable as well. Big as he was, he was quite docile. Mickey was a differ-ent kettle of fish. I suppose he had to be. In Ballymurphy small dogs live very combative lives, especially small small ones like Mickey.

When the British Army arrived on the scene my visits home became more infrequent. At times I may only have been a few streets or even only a few houses away but 1970 and '71 weren't actually great dog-walking years, so Shane and I cut down on our excursions. I still saw him, of course. Our Liam or our Sean would walk him down to wherever I was and we would have an hour or so together. The problem was that when it was time to part Shane used to go wild. He would rear up on his hind legs, crying and shouting and barking and yelping. It got so that our Liam or our Sean could hardly hold him as he jerked away from them, pulling and straining on his lead and bawling out to me. In a way it used to please me, I suppose. Once I got a week off and we spent our time wandering through the fields of Aughyneill down south, far away from British Army patrols, but he fretted for days on returning to Belfast when we went our separate ways again.

In 1971 the Brits killed Mickey. They killed a lot of dogs in Ballymurphy. The dogs gave an early warning that the Brits were in the area. The dogs used to give them gyp and with our house being raided so often Mickey would go crazy whenever he caught sight or scent of a British soldier. After they killed him our Dominic cried for a week.

Then in 1973 Shane vanished. The Brits took him, of course. Somebody saw him up in the Henry Taggart British Army base but there was nothing we could do. My Ma phoned the barracks and complained but of course it was pointless. We had always been afraid that the Brits would get him—they are always keen to get any half-decent dog. They had tried to take Shane before, but my Da caught them and got him back. This time, though, we didn't get him back. I was in Long Kesh by then, interned in Cage 6.

We used to get very frequent British Army raids in the cage; at times they even raided us twice in one night. Usually they raided at about half-four in the morning. They would sneak into the huts, slipping into place at the foot of our beds and then, as the one in charge snapped on the lights, they all beat hell out of the beds with their batons.

"This is a British Army search!" one of them would scream at us. "When told to do so, you will take your knife, fork and spoon and go to the canteen."

We would be escorted one at a time through a gauntlet of British troops to spend the morning in an empty hut. Sometimes we would be put on the wire, legs and arms and fingers splayed wide and holding the body weight. It was hard going, especially at half-four in the morning. After the first hour you forgot what end of you was up.

One morning we got a Brit raid which was no big deal. They took it easy enough and none of us wanted any trouble. When the raid was over we were taken back from the canteen to our hut, one at a time as was the routine, through two lines of British soldiers. Sometimes some of the Brits would slabber at us or use their batons and occasionally they would "seize" their war-dogs, setting them on us. This particular morning nothing untoward happened and the worst we were hit with were the usual and predictable insults.

Just as I turned the corner of our hut I saw Shane. He was about fifty yards from me, close to the gate of the cage, and accompanied by a small, stocky British Army dog-handler.

I had about ten yards to walk. Our Shane was clearly in my view. I shouted out to him but he didn't move. Then I whistled, the way I always whistled for him: one long, three short, then one long whistle, all in the one breath.

He tensed immediately, ears cocked, head alert, his body on point. Jesus, he was a smashing-looking dog!

"You! Fuck up!" the Brit nearest me said.

I whistled again and slowed my pace. Our Shane saw me just as I reached the end of the hut. He jerked towards me and the Brit dog-handler, just like our Liam and Sean before him, could hardly hold him. Shane was rearing up on his hind legs, crying and shouting, barking and yelling. I thought he was going to break free as he lunged forward, jerking away from his handler, pulling and straining on his lead and howling out to me.

Then a Brit shoved me around the corner and into our hut. I could still hear Shane crying. The lads behind me told me that he had to be taken out of our cage, still pulling and straining against his handler. And still crying.

Phases

DON'T TALK TO ME LIKE THAT!"
"Like what?"
Jimmy Brady looked at his son. He leaned back in his chair and sucked his breath in in sharp little gasps before exhaling in a long, loud, frustrated sigh. He made a face, placed both his hands on the table as if to steady himself and then, raising his head slowly, he looked at Sean once more. When he spoke this time his tone was even, placatory.

"Look, son, this is getting none of us anywhere. You mightn't realize it but your attitude leaves a lot to be desired. Every time I try to talk to you it ends up in an argument. I'm sick of it. You'll have to learn to take things easy."

Sean remained silent. He stared sullenly at his father; then anger flared for a second in his eyes. Words flowed out in an angry torrent.

"Why is it always me has to take things easy? I can't do anything these days without you giving off to me. You're never off my back! You're sick of it? How do you think I feel?"

They were seated, facing each other across the dinner table. Jimmy could feel the temper rising inside him. Once again he strove to remain calm. But when Sean pointed his finger at him he snapped.

"Don't do that! How many times have I to tell you not to talk to me like that?"

He kicked his chair back and leaned across the table, towering over Sean. "I'm your father and I deserve more respect than this from you. I'd be better off falling in drunk every night, abusing your mother and gambling away my wages. You'd think more of me then, wouldn't you?"

He was shouting at the top of his voice. As Sean rose to face him Mary rushed in from the kitchen where she was preparing the evening meal. "What in the name of God's wrong now? Yis have the place like a madhouse. What's the matter with the two of yous? Yis are like two wee children!"

"That's right, Ma, you pick on me as well!" Sean retorted, stepping away from the table to face both his parents.

"I'm no wee child, Mary. I'm his father and he'll not behave like that in my house," Jimmy protested. "It's you has him the way he is. And you . . ." he turned on Sean again: "that's no way to talk to your mother. I don't want another word out of you."

"It's a pity I'm not a dummy isn't it? You'd be happy then, wouldn't you?"

"Sean, shut your mouth!"

"What'll you do if I don't? Eh? What'll you do? Put me to bed early! I'm no wee kid, Da. You can't boss me about any longer."

"Sean," his mother interrupted him, "Sean, please. Please sit down and have your dinner."

"No, Ma. I'm going down to Mickey's. I know where I'm not welcome."

"Ach, Sean," Mary pleaded, "don't be going out without your dinner. Jimmy, get him to stay. This is not right, a father and son getting on like this. Jimmy, please. You should have more sense. You never give the lad an earthly."

"That's what's wrong in this house, woman," Jimmy yelled at her.

He left his place at the table and advanced towards Sean who defiantly stood his ground in the center of the room. Mary rushed between them. She faced her husband, pushing him in the chest as she screamed at her son.

"That's enough, Sean. Go on away down to Mickey's. You can get your dinner later."

Sean rushed from the room, choking on his tears. "I don't want any dinner," he shouted.

Jimmy strained against his wife, but she stood firm. He turned from her in disgust.

"Dinner, I'd give him dinner! It's a good toe up the hole he wants and not sympathy from you. It's you has him the way he is. I'm sick telling you not to take his part. How do you expect him to pay any heed to me when you keep butting in and undermining me?" Jimmy slumped on to the settee by the fire. He buried his face in his hands.

"I'm sick of it," he said.

Mary knelt beside him.

"I'm sick of it too," she said. "I don't know what I'm going to do with the two of yous." She took his hands in hers. They hung together in silence until eventually Mary eased herself up off her knees.

"You've me murdered," she joked, tousling his hair. "I've a cramp in my thigh."

She rubbed her leg energetically. "Come on and cheer up," she told him. "Your dinner will be freezing."

"I don't want any, Mary," Jimmy said moodily, "I don't feel like eating just now."

"Well, I don't know what to do to please yous. I rushed in early to make sure the two of yous got. . ."

Jimmy interrupted her with a fierceness which took her aback.

"There you go again, woman. It's not the two of us. I'm not the same as Sean. He's only fifteen. I'm his father. You're always going on about 'the two of us.' That's some way to instill discipline in him, isn't it? He doesn't do a hand's turn around the house. He leaves everything at his arse. He treats the place like a hotel and you, more fool anyway, you're like his servant, and the only time he speaks to me is to be cheeky or to ask for something. And what's your answer to it all?"

He looked at her with contempt.

"You talk about the two of us as if me and him were two wee lads who fell out. It's no wonder he's the way he is!"

Mary fought back the tears.

"Why don't you try talking to him?" she said. "You were never like this with our Damian or Joseph when they were Sean's age."

"They never got on like him," Jimmy retorted. "They weren't spoiled."

"And Sean's not spoiled either," Mary continued. "No more than any of the rest of them. He's not a bad lad. He's just going through a wee phase. You can't expect him to be any different than all the others. It's just that he's the youngest and the only one here, and he thinks he's a big fella now. Why don't you and him have a wee talk. It can't go on like this. I can't cope with it."

She could hold back the tears no longer. As she turned sobbing and retreated into the kitchen, Jimmy softened. He followed her in and took her in his arms.

"I'm sorry," he said. "Don't be crying. I'll talk to Sean when he comes in. All right?"

Sean was slightly smaller than his father but by the way he was growing Jimmy guessed that it wouldn't be long until he was dwarfed by his youngest son. Sean was taller already than his older brothers. "That's maybe why I'm so sore on him," Jimmy reflected. "He looks much older than he is and I'm probably expecting him to behave like someone older."

They were sitting together in the living room watching the football on television. It was the Saturday after the big row. In the two days since then barely a word had passed between them. Mary was out shopping. On her way out she had whispered to Jimmy as he stood in the hallway waiting to lock the front door after her, "Now's the time for you and Sean to have a wee yarn."

Jimmy knew she was right. He had always been able to talk to his children. He and Sean had actually enjoyed a special relationship, mostly, as Mary said, because he gave Sean the time he hadn't been able to give the others. They had got on great until about nine months ago. Since then, Jimmy smiled wryly to himself, it had been a murder picture.

He glanced across at Sean. "H'y doing, son?"

"I'm all right."

"Sean, son, it's about time we had a wee yarn. I've been..."

"It's a bit late to be thinking about a wee yarn now, Da, isn't it?" Sean interrupted him gruffly.

"What do y' mean?" Jimmy was just as gruff.

They looked directly at one another.

"Look, Sean," Jimmy said, "I only want us to talk. Now, if you don't want to talk that's fair enough. But we'll have to talk sometime. We can't go on not talking or bawling at one another all the time. So it's up to you. I'm not going to coax you and I'm certainly not going to fight with you. This is my day off and I've better things to do. So what do you say?"

"Okay," Sean conceded sullenly, "we'll talk."

"You'll have to do better than that," Jimmy smiled patiently. "Let's start by making friends." He reached his hand out to Sean, who hesitated only for an instant before grasping his father's hand in a warm, firm handshake. They both smiled.

"That's better," Jimmy smiled. "Do you fancy a cup of tea?"

"Aye, Da, I don't mind if I do. Like, you don't have to go overboard."

"I'll tell you what, Sean. Do you see, every boy. . ." Jimmy paused for a minute as he concentrated on squeezing the last drop of brown moisture from the teabags.

"There you are." He pushed a cup over to Sean. They were standing in the kitchen. Sean was buttering toast. He put a few slices on a plate for his father and they adjourned again to the living room.

"Where was I?" Jimmy asked him through a mouthful of hot toast.

"You were about to give me one of your fatherly talks," Sean said.

"You'd do it with a bit more dignity if you hadn't a big blob of butter dribbling down your chin. Will I get you a bib?" he laughed.

"Somebody swallowed a dictionary. Dignity? That's a new word for you."

Jimmy wiped his chin and waited until his son's laughter ceased.

"What I was about to say was that every boy goes through certain phases with his father. Phase number one is when his father is a hero. He can do no wrong. No other boy's father is half as good as yours. He can outrun, outthink and beat just everybody else at everything. You know what I mean?"

Jimmy smiled at Sean a little self-consciously.

"You know, like, up to the time when you start school and for a few years after that."

Sean shifted in his seat.

"Well," his father continued as he finished off the last of the toast, "as I said, that's phase number one. Phase number two comes much later. That's when every boy wonders how he could have been cursed with such an awful Da. That happens to every boy also. You know what I mean. Your Da picks on you all the time. He embarrasses you in front of your friends. He thinks he knows everything and that you know nothing. He treats you like a child. Well, that's the second phase. Phase number three? Phase number three is the last phase. That's when the boy becomes a man and realizes that his Da is just the same as him."

Jimmy handed his empty cup to Sean.

"That's the three phases, son," he concluded. "And now that we're muckers again, do you think you could get your oul' lad a wee taste of tea and another round of that toast, seeing as you ate the most of it."

Sean grinned as he took the cup.

"No problem, Da," he said. "No problem."

Mary knew that things would be back to normal again when she returned home. Her only worry was that Sean wouldn't give Jimmy the chance to talk to him, but she thought that was unlikely. The way the two of them were behaving after two days of not talking it was only a matter of someone breaking the ice, and she was sure Jimmy would do that. For all their annoyance at each other Mary knew none of them enjoyed the breakdown in their relationship.

Sean met her in the hall and took the trio of bulging plastic shopping bags from her.

"All right, Ma?" he said. "I hope you've something nice there for me; me Da's ate all the bread and I'm starving."

"Is that right, son?" Despite her optimism, she conceded a wee sigh of relief.

She followed Sean into the kitchen where his father was busily washing the dishes.

"Ah, Mary," he greeted her, "just in time to make us a big fry."

"Bloody men!" she answered good-humoredly. "I suppose yous would've starved if I hadn't come back. What would yous do if I ran away?"

Later, as all three of them bustled about the kitchen preparing the meal, she turned to Jimmy.

"I suppose you think you're great now that you and your son are talking again," she said quietly.

"Indeed I do," he grinned.

"So do I," she agreed.

That's the way it was for about a fortnight. All peace and harmony. Then one Wednesday evening when Jimmy came in the door from work Sean rushed past him in the hall and charged upstairs. When he came back down Jimmy was seated at the fire with his dinner on a tray on his knee.

"You're like a herd of elephants going up the stairs," he said.

"She left my jeans up there," Sean replied sulkily, making his way past his father to the kitchen. He had his jeans in his hand.

"Who's she?" Jimmy asked.

There was no reply. Sean had gone on into the kitchen and didn't hear his father.

"Who's she?" Jimmy asked again, louder and with an edge to his voice. Silence. He put his tray on the floor in front of him.

"Sean!" he yelled. Still no response. The kitchen door opened.

Jimmy, halfway out of his chair, could hear Sean and his mother talking in the kitchen.

"Sean!" he yelled.

"What on earth's the matter?" Mary's tone was annoyed. That irritated Jimmy even more.

"I was talking to him and he walked right past me," he snapped. "Sean."

"What, Da?" Sean's voice was heavy with sarcasm.

"Don't 'what-Da' me." Jimmy was on his feet. "Who's she?" he confronted Sean.

"What?"

"Don't 'what' me, Sean. I'm not an eejit. Who's she? Is that any way to talk to your mother?"

"I don't know what you're on about," said Sean.

"Don't mess with me, Sean," Jimmy yelled at him.

Sean exploded.

"Don't mess with you! You're the one that's doing all the messing. I'm sick of this." He turned to his mother. "I'm sick of this, Ma! He's never off my back."

Jimmy was almost beside himself with rage now.

"Who's she?" he roared. "You need to be taught a bit of respect."

"I'm trying to go out, Da," Sean roared back. "You. . ."

"You'll go out when I tell you and not before," his father interrupted.

"Is that right," Sean shouted. "Well then, I'll not go out at all! I'm away up the stairs, Ma." He brushed past his father.

"Sean!" Jimmy commanded.

Sean ignored him and rushed from the room, slamming the door in his wake.

"Jesus, give me patience!" Jimmy cried.

He sat back heavily in his seat. His dinner, growing cold on the tray, lay ignored at his feet. He looked up at Mary.

"Take it easy, Jimmy," she said. "I don't know about you, but I can't take much more of this. You want to watch your temper," she concluded as she, too, left the room.

Upstairs she confronted Sean.

"Go you down the stairs this minute and apologize to your father."

"Why should I apologize to him?" Sean was lying on his bed. She could see he had been crying. He looked at her indignantly as he spoke.

"Because I said so," Mary heard herself say. The words were out of her before she realized it, words she had heard so often from her own parents, words she had promised herself she would never use to her own children. Now having said them she was committed. "Sean. I'm not going to let this go on a minute longer."

"You always take his side."

"Sean, I'm not putting up with any of your oul' nonsense. Get up, wash your face and don't take all night about it, and then go down and see your Da."

She paused for a minute. Sean sat up and edged to the side of the bed. She tousled his hair with her hand.

"Come on," she coaxed him. "You and your Da shouldn't be fighting. Go and see him before things get worse and then when you've made the peace, go on out like you planned. Okay?"

Sean started to protest.

"Sean, please," she silenced him. "Do it for me. Please."

Sean rolled his eyes and sighed resignedly. "Okay, Ma."

"Good boy," she said.

Downstairs she faced her husband. He looked at her sullenly.

"Jimmy, Sean's sorry about losin' his temper. He's coming down now to talk to you. Try and be patient. He was rushing to go out. Let him make peace and go on out."

"Mary, I'm only in after working hard all day. He can't. . ." Jimmy started to protest.

"Jimmy, please," she silenced him. "Do it for me. Please."

Jimmy looked at her for a long, silent minute.

"Please," she repeated.

"Okay, love."

"Give's your dinner," she said. "I'll heat it up for you. Here he comes now. Take it easy, won't you?" She smiled anxiously at him.

"Okay." Despite himself he smiled back at her. "Don't worry."

"Thanks, love."

She took the tray from him and as she did she touched him lightly on the cheek. She headed for the kitchen as Sean's footsteps were heard on the stairs. He walked hesitantly into the living room to his father.

"I'm sorry, Da," he said.

Jimmy stared at him for an instant.

"I don't know what gets into you, son."

"I said I'm sorry, Da," Sean repeated uncomfortably.

Jimmy got up slowly from his seat. He offered Sean his hand.

"Okay, son," he said. "We'll let it go for tonight."

Sean took his father's hand.

"I am sorry, Da," he repeated.

"Dead on, Sean," Jimmy forgave him. "Let it go. I was a bit under pressure myself."

The tension between them was broken.

"We'll have to stop fighting, son."

"I know, Da. I'm going to go on out. Is that all right?"

"No problem. By the way, son," Jimmy was teasing, "what was wrong with you? Is your lovelife not going right?"

Sean had turned to go. With his hand on the doorknob he paused and looked back at Jimmy.

"No, Da. My lovelife's dead on. I'm just going through phase two."

Does He Take Sugar?

TOM MACAULEY, youngest son of Martha and Joe MacAuley, was nineteen years old. Joe worked in the office of a Derry shirt factory and he, Martha and Tom lived not far from the Strand Road.

Tom, who had Down's Syndrome, had been born ten years after his four brothers and three sisters, and when they had all left home to get married or to seek work abroad Tom had remained to become the center of his parents' lives. Already in her late forties when Tom had been born, Martha's health was starting to fail by the time he had reached his teens. But when he wasn't at school Tom rarely left his mother's side.

"Poor Mrs. MacAuley," the neighbors would say when she and young Tom passed by. "She never gets a minute to herself. That young Tom is a handful, God look to him. Morning, noon and night he's always with his mother. She never gets a break."

Tom attended a special school and when he was sixteen, the year his father retired from the shirt factory, he graduated to a special project at a day center on Northland Road. A bus collected him each morning at the corner and brought him back each evening. His father escorted him to the bus and was there again in the evening faithfully awaiting his return.

Tom loved the day center. He called it work and it was work of a sort; each week he was paid £3.52 for framing pictures. He also had many new friends and was constantly falling in and out of love with a number of girls who worked with him. Geraldine was his special favorite but he was forced to admire her from afar; she never gave any indication that she was even aware of his existence. His relationships with the others never really flourished, but at least with them he wasn't as invisible as he was with Geraldine. He could enjoy their company and one of them, Margaret Begley, wasn't a bit backward about letting him know that she had a crush on him. Tom gave her no encouragement: his heart was with Geraldine. Anyway, he was too shy for Margaret's extrovert ways.

Tom's parents knew nothing of all his feelings towards the girls, but they knew that the work was good for him. At times he would return home excited or annoyed by something which had occurred at the day center, and when this happened Martha knew the instant she saw him. When he was excited, perhaps from having had a trip to the pictures or when his supervisor praised his work in front of everyone, he radiated happiness. When he was annoyed, he stammered furiously.

On these occasions he rarely volunteered information and Martha and Joe soon learned that it was useless to question him. Under interrogation he would remain stubbornly noncommittal and if pressed he became resentful and agitated. Left to his own devices, though, he would reveal, in his own time, usually by his own series of questions, the source of his discontent. Tom's questions followed a pattern.

"MMMM Ma," he would say, "DDD Does Mick Mick Mickey BBBBradley know how how how to dddddrive a cacaacar?"

"No, son, Mickey wouldn't be allowed to drive a car."

"Hhhhehe says he cacacan."

"He's keeping you going, Tom."

"If we had a cacacar could I drdrdrive it?"

"Of course," Martha would smile. "Your Daddy would teach you."

"Right," Tom would say, and that would be that.

Work gave Tom a small but important measure of independence and his experiences at work rarely impinged on his home life. Martha and Joe's relationship with him remained largely as it had been before. They still never permitted him to go off alone, except in his own street. Tom didn't seem to mind. He collected postcards. When he was at home he spent most of his time counting and recounting, sorting and resorting his collection in scrapbooks and old shoeboxes and writing down their serial numbers in jotters which his father bought him.

He also did small chores around the house. It was his job to keep the coal-bucket filled and he always cleared the table after dinner. Occasionally he helped with the dishes and he fetched dusters and polish or things like that for his mother when she did her cleaning. Most mornings he also collected the paper in the corner shop while his mother prepared the breakfast. Seamus Hughes the shopkeeper always delighted him with his greeting.

"Ah, Tom, you'll be wanting to catch up on the news. Here's your paper."

Tom would be especially happy if there was anyone else in the shop to hear Seamus's remarks. He would beam with pleasure and mumble his red-faced and affirmative response.

His father and he went for walks regularly every Saturday and Sunday afternoon and Tom loved these outings. His usual facial expression was blandly benign but when he smiled he smiled with his whole face, and during the walks with his father the smile rarely left him. Everyone knew the pair and had a friendly greeting for them both. Usually they walked out the line where the doggymen exercised their greyhounds, and on one memorable Sunday they took the back road across the border and went the whole way as far as Doherty's Fort at the Grianán of Aileach in Donegal. The following day was the only occasion on which Tom missed work; he was so tired after their outing that Martha couldn't rouse him from the bed. His father joked with him about it afterwards.

At Christmas there was a pantomime at Tom's work. Tom had a small part as Aladdin's servant. All the parents and families along with various agencies and local dignitaries were invited to the center for an open night. Samples of handicrafts were on display and photographs of their projects adorned the walls. On the night of the performance when the audience were milling around in the main corridor sipping tea and lemonade while they waited for the show to start in the main hall, one of Tom's workmates, a young man from the Brandywell called Hughie, suddenly started yelling and bawling.

At first everyone just looked away and pretended that nothing was amiss but as Hughie's parents failed to pacify him the commotion increased. One of the supervisors intervened but that only seemed to make Hughie worse. Apparently this was the first year that Hughie had not had a part in the pantomime. When rehearsals had begun earlier in the year he had insisted that he didn't want a part. Now when he saw the gathering and the excitement of his friends as they prepared for the evening's performance and when it was too late for him to do anything, he had changed his mind. He wanted to be in the pantomime and nothing would satisfy him except that.

His parents were distracted and as Hughie continued his bad-tempered hysterics their consternation spread to the audience. Some of the pantomime players came from the big hall, where they were nervously finalizing last-minute arrangements, to see what the racket was about. Tom was among them, dressed in an oriental-type outfit made by his mother from old curtains and an old dressing gown.

No one paid much attention when Tom left his costumed friends and made his way through the throng to where Hughie stood bawling in the corner, surrounded by his distraught parents and two of the day center supervisors. Then to everyone's surprise Tom intervened.

"Ex-cuse me," he said to Hughie's parents, and without waiting for a reply he pushed his way past them before stopping with his face close to Hughie's.

"Shughie, ddddddon't be be ge ge gett-ing on like th th this," he stammered.

Hughie ignored him. Tom looked at his friend beseechingly. Hughie still ignored him and carried on bawling.

Tom leaned over and whispered in Hughie's ear, then stopped and looked at him again. Hughie continued to bawl but less stridently now. Tom leaned over and whispered again in his ear. Hughie stopped. Tom looked at him once more.

"All rrrright?" he asked.

Hughie nodded.

Tom turned and walked back to his friends. As they watched him Martha and Joe were as pleased as Punch, especially when Tom's supervisor came over and shook their hands.

"That's a great lad you have there. He's a credit to the two of you the way he handled Hughie."

After the pantomime Hughie's father was equally lavish in his praise.

"I'm really grateful for the way your Tom quietened down our Hughie. It's wonderful the way they can communicate with each other in a way that the rest of us can't. Your Tom's the proof of that. The way he was able to get through to our Hughie. None of the rest of us could do that. It never fails to amaze me. Tom's a great lad."

On the way home that night Joe asked Tom what he had said to Hughie. Tom was pleased with all the attention he was receiving but he was noncommittal about his conversation with Hughie. When Joe pressed the issue Tom got a little edgy. Martha squeezed Joe's arm authoritatively.

"Leave things as they are," she whispered.

Joe nudged Tom.

"I'm not allowed to ask you anything else!" he joked.

Tom smiled at him.

"That's good," he said.

Over the Christmas holidays all Tom's brothers and sisters visited home. Tom especially enjoyed his nephews and nieces and the way they brought the house alive with their shouting and laughing, crying and fighting.

A few days after Christmas Martha's sister Crissie came to visit them as she always did. During her visits Tom spent a lot of time in his room sorting his postcards. He was in the living room when Aunt Crissie arrived—his mother insisted on that—but after the flurry of greetings had subsided Tom made his escape. A retired schoolteacher and a spinster, the oldest of Martha's sisters, Aunt Crissie tended to fuss around him, and this made him uneasy. Joe shared his son's unease in the presence of Aunt Crissie, thinking her a busybody but all the same marveling at her energy and clearness of mind.

"I hope I'm as sprightly as that when I get to her age," he would say to whoever was listening.

Crissie hugged Tom and held him at arms' length for a full inspection. "Tommy's looking great, Martha," she said.

She always called Tom Tommy. He shifted from foot to foot and gave her his best grin.

"Thhhh tank th thank thank you, Aunt CiciciCrisssssie."

"I've-brought-you-a-little-something-for-your-stocking, Tommy."

When Aunt Crissie spoke to Tom directly she did so very slowly. She also raised her voice a little. She always brought him two pairs of socks.

"Thhhh tank th thank thank you, Aunt CiciciCrissssie."

"Away you go now, Tom," his mother said.

Tom and his father usually went off together for a while before their dinner, the highlight of Aunt Crissie's visit. By that time Crissie and Martha were in full flow on a year of family gossip. This continued through the dinner of tasty Christmas Day leftovers until, appetite and curiosity satisfied, Aunt Crissie turned her attention again to Tom. She had poured the tea and was handing around the milk and sugar.

"Does he take sugar?" she asked Joe.

"Do you, Tom?" Joe redirected the question to his son.

"Nnno, Da," Tom replied in surprise.

Martha looked sharply at her husband. Aunt Crissie saw the glance and apologized quickly.

"I'm-sorry, Tommy. Of-course-you-don't. I-remember-now. Your-mother-tells-me-you're-getting-on-very-well-at-the-day-center."

"Aaayye, I am."

Joe intervened. He was anxious to smooth things over.

"Tom was in the pantomime. It was a great night. They've a great team of people involved with that center. And all the kids love it. Tom really likes it down there. And he has plenty of friends."

"It must be very rewarding work for the people involved," Crissie suggested. She, too, was anxious that the awkwardness be forgotten.

"Tom's supervisor says she wouldn't work with any other kids," Martha said. "We were talking to her after the pantomime and she said that Down's Syndrome cases are the easiest to work with."

"They retain the innocence and trust that the rest of us lose," said Joe, "and you know something, they are well able to communicate with one another in a way the rest of us will probably never understand. Isn't that right, Tom?"

Tom looked up from his tea and smiled blankly at his father.

"Wait till you hear this, Crissie," Joe continued. "Before the pantomime another lad, Hughie, a friend of Tom's, threw a tantrum and the only one who could calm him down was Tom. It just goes to show you. Nobody else could get through to him; then Tom spoke quietly to him and the next thing Hughie was as right as rain. Isn't that right, Martha?"

Martha took up the story from there and recounted the pantomime night episode. When she was finished Aunt Crissie turned to Tom.

"Well done, young man. It's wonderful that you were able to do that. What did you say, by the way?"

Joe chuckled.

"That's something we'll never know. Eh, Tom?"

"Och, Tommy, you can tell us," Aunt Crissie persisted.

Tom lowered his head and shifted self-consciously in his chair.

"C'mon, Tom," his mother encouraged him.

He looked up at them. Aunt Crissie was smiling at him.

"Is he going to say something?" she asked.

Tom looked towards her. He was frowning. Then slowly his face smiled as it was taken over by one of his huge grins. He looked at his father, as if for encouragement, before turning again to Aunt Crissie.

"I told him I would knock his balls in if he didn't stop messing about," he said slowly and without a single stutter. "Shughie'sss spoiled. All he needed was a gggood dig. That's all I sa sa said to hhhiim him."

Martha, Joe and Aunt Crissie were speechless. Tom looked at each of them in turn, a little hesitantly at first. Then as his father winked slowly at him the bland, benign expression returned to his face. Joe started to laugh.

Tom's anxiety vanished and his face lit up at the sound. He looked again at his mother and Aunt Crissie and began to laugh also as he watched the looks on their faces. He turned again to his father and winked slowly in return.

A Life Before Death?

T
HE WHITEROCK ROAD was pitch black and the occasional young couple, hurrying home, clung their way past McCrory Park.

A few stragglers leaned together outside Jim's Cafe. An overcrowded black taxi labored up the hill. Few people noticed the two figures walking down towards the Falls Road. One was a thickset man in black overcoat, white open-necked shirt and white drill trousers. He wore a cap pushed back on his head, and walked with one hand in his pocket. He didn't seem to be in any hurry. His companion, a younger man dressed in jeans and an anorak, had to shorten his natural stride to match the older man's. They walked in silence alongside the cemetery wall until they reached the Falls Road. They turned right at the bottom of the Whiterock and strolled slowly up the road. The young man cleared his throat. His companion glanced at him.

"Come on, we'll cut down here."

The younger man nodded. They hurried down Milltown Row and went more cautiously then, the older man in front bent forward with one hand still in his pocket. Down and over the football pitch, across the Bog Meadows and up towards the graveyard.

The moon peeked out at them from behind clouds. Cars on the motorway below sped by unknowing and uncaring. The man with the cap was out of breath by the time they reached the hedge at Milltown Cemetery. The cemetery waited on them, rows and rows of serried tombstones reflecting the cold moonlight. It was desperately quiet. Even the sounds from the motorway and the road seemed cut off, subdued. They forced their way through the hedge and on to the tarmac pathway. Nothing stirred. They waited a few tense seconds and then moved off, silently, a little apart, the young man in the rear, the man with the cap in front. It was twenty past eleven.

The young man's heart thumped heavily against his ribs. He was glad he wasn't alone, though he wished the older man hadn't worn the white trousers. They wouldn't be long now anyway. Ahead of them lay their destination. As the moon came from behind a cloud he could see the pathway stretching before him. His companion cut across a grassy bank and the young man, relaxing a little by now, continued on alone for the last few yards.

He thought of the morning when they had last been there, the funeral winding its way down from the Whiterock, the people crossing themselves as it passed, the guard of honor awkward but solemn around the hearse. He thought of the people who had crowded around the graveside. Men and women long used to hardship but still shocked at the suddenness of death. Young people and old people. Friends of the family, neighbors and comrades of the deceased. United in their grief. And in their anger too, he reflected.

He sighed softly, almost inaudibly, to himself as he came alongside his companion again. The older man whispered to him. Wreaths lay on the grave which had been dug that morning and the fresh clay glistened where the diggers had shaped it into a ridge. The two men glanced at each other and then, silently, they stood abreast of the grave.

They prayed their silent prayers and the moon, spying from above, hid behind a cloud. The men stood to attention. A night wind crept down from the Black Mountain and rustled through the wreaths. The older man barked an order. They both raised revolvers towards the sky and three volleys of shots crashed over the grave.

The young man was tense, a little pale. The man with the cap breathed freely. He pocketed his weapon. The young man shoved his into the waistband of his jeans. They moved off quickly. The moon slid from behind the clouds, the wind shook itself and swept across the landscape. All was quiet once more. The two men, moving across the fields, reached the Falls Road. They walked slowly; they didn't seem to be in any hurry. Few people noticed them as they walked up the Whiterock Road. It was five past twelve. Jim's Cafe was closed. An occasional young couple, hurrying home, clung their way past McCrory Park. A car coming out of Whiterock Drive stopped to let the two men cross its path. As they did so the cemetery wall was caught in the car's headlights.

The white graffitied "IS THERE A LIFE BEFORE DEATH?" flashed as the vehicle swung on to the main road and headed off towards Ballymurphy.

The two men paused and looked at each other. Then they, too, continued on their journey.

A Good Confession

T HE CONGREGATION SHUFFLED its feet. An old man
spluttered noisily into his handkerchief, his body racked by
a spasm of coughing. He wiped his nose wearily and
returned to his prayers. A small child cried bad-temperedly in its
mother's arms. Embarrassed, she released him into the side aisle of
the chapel where, shoes clattering on the marble floor, he ran excitedly back and forth. His mother stared intently at the altar and tried
to distance herself from her irreverent infant. He never even noticed
her indifference; his attention was consumed by the sheer joy of
being free and soon he was trying to cajole another restless child to
join him in the aisle. Another wave of coughing wheezed through the
adult worshippers. As if encouraged by such solidarity the old man
resumed his catarrhal cacophony.

The priest leaned forward in the pulpit and directed himself and
his voice towards his congregation. As he spoke they relaxed as he
knew they would. Only the children, absorbed in their innocence,
continued as before. Even the old man, by some superhuman effort,
managed to control his phlegm.

"My dear brothers and sisters," the priest began. "It is a matter of deep distress and worry to me and I'm sure to you also that there are some Catholics who have so let the eyes of their soul become darkened that they no longer recognize sin as sin."

He paused for a second or so to let his words sink in. He was a young man, not bad looking in an ascetic sort of a way, Mrs. McCarthy thought, especially when he was intense about something, as he was now. She was in her usual seat at the side of the church and as she waited for Fr. Burns to continue his sermon she thought to herself that it was good to have a new young priest in the parish.

Fr. Burns cleared his throat and continued.

"I'm talking about the evil presence we have in our midst and I'm asking you, the God-fearing people of this parish, to join with me in this Eucharist in praying that we loosen from the neck of our society the grip which a few have tightened around it and from which we sometimes despair of ever being freed."

He stopped again momentarily. The congregation was silent: he had their attention. Even the sounds from the children were muted.

"I ask you all to pray with me that eyes that have become blind may be given sight, consciences that have become hardened and closed may be touched by God and opened to the light of His truth and love. I am speaking of course of the men of violence." He paused, leant forward on arched arms, and continued.

"I am speaking of the IRA and its fellow-travelers. This community of ours has suffered much in the past. I know that. I do not doubt but that in the IRA organization there are those who entered the movement for idealistic reasons. They need to ask themselves now where that idealism has led them. We Catholics need to be quite clear about this."

Fr. Burns sensed that he was losing the attention of his flock again. The old man had lost or given up the battle to control his coughing. Others shuffled uneasily in their seats. A child shrieked excitedly at the back of the church. Some like Mrs. McCarthy still listened intently and he resolved to concentrate on them.

"Membership, participation in or cooperation with the IRA and its military operations is most gravely sinful. Now I know that I am a new priest here and some of you may be wondering if I am being political when I say these things. I am not. I am preaching Catholic moral teaching and I can only say that those who do not listen are cutting themselves off from the community of the Church. They cannot sincerely join with their fellow Catholics who gather at mass and pray in union with the whole Church. Let us all as we pray together, let us all resolve that we will never cut ourselves off from God in this way and let us pray for those who do."

Fr. Burns paused for the last time before concluding.

"In the name of the Father and the Son and the Holy Ghost."

Just after Communion and before the end of the mass there was the usual trickling exit of people out of the church. When Fr. Burns gave the final blessing the trickle became a flood. Mrs. McCarthy stayed in her seat. It was her custom to say a few prayers at Our Lady's altar before going home. She waited for the crowd to clear.

Jinny Blake, a neighbor, stopped on her way up the aisle and leaned confidentially towards her. "Hullo, Mrs. McCarthy," she whispered reverently, her tone in keeping with their surroundings.

"Hullo, Jinny. You're looking well, so you are."

"I'm doing grand, thank God. You're looking well yourself. Wasn't that new wee priest just lovely? And he was like lightning too. It makes a change to get out of twelve o'clock mass so quickly."

"Indeed it does," Mrs. McCarthy agreed as she and Jinny whispered their goodbyes.

By now the chapel was empty except for a few older people who stayed behind, like Mrs. McCarthy, to say their special prayers or to light blessed candles. Mrs. McCarthy left her seat and made her way slowly towards the small side altar. She genuflected awkwardly as she passed the sanctuary. As she did so the new priest came out from the sacristy. He had removed his vestments and dressed in his dark suit he looked slighter than she had imagined him to be when he had been saying mass.

"Hullo," he greeted her.

"Hullo, Father, welcome to Saint Jude's."

His boyish smile made her use of the term "Father" seem incongruous.

"Thank you," he said.

"By the way, Father. . ."

The words were out of her in a rush before she knew it.

"I didn't agree with everything you said in your sermon. Surely if you think those people are sinners you should be welcoming them into the Church and not chasing them out of it."

Fr. Burns was taken aback. "I was preaching Church teaching," he replied a little sharply.

It was a beautiful morning. He had been very nervous about the sermon, his first in a new parish. He had put a lot of thought into it and now when it was just over him and his relief had scarcely subsided he was being challenged by an old woman.

Mrs. McCarthy could feel his disappointment and resentment. She had never spoken like this before, especially to a priest. She retreated slightly. "I'm sorry, Father," she said uncomfortably, "I just thought you were a bit hard." She sounded apologetic. Indeed, as she looked at the youth of him she regretted that she had opened her mouth at all.

Fr. Burns was blushing slightly as he searched around for a response.

"Don't worry," he said finally, "I'm glad you spoke your mind. But you have to remember I was preaching God's word and there's no arguing with that."

They walked slowly up the center aisle towards the main door. Fr. Burns was relaxed now. He had one hand on her elbow and as he spoke he watched her with a faint little smile on his lips. Despite herself she felt herself growing angry at his presence. Who was this young man almost steering her out of the chapel? She hadn't even been at Our Lady's altar yet.

"We have to choose between our politics and our religion," he was saying.

"That's fair enough, Father, as far as it goes, but I think it's wrong to chase people away from the church," she began.

91

"They do that themselves," he interrupted her.

She saw that he still had that little smile. They were almost at the end of the aisle. She stopped sharply, surprising the priest as she did, so that he stopped also and stood awkwardly with his hand still on her elbow.

"I'm sorry, Father, I'm not going out yet."

It was his turn to be flustered and she noticed with some satisfaction that his smile had disappeared. Before he could recover she continued, "I still think it's wrong to exclude people. Who are any of us to judge anyone, to say who is or who isn't a good Catholic, or a good Christian for that matter? I know them that lick the altar rails and, God forgive me, they wouldn't give you a drink of water if you were dying of the thirst. No, Father, it's not all black and white. You'll learn that before you're much older."

His face reddened at her last remark.

"The Church is quite clear in its teaching on the issue of illegal organizations. Catholics cannot support or be a part of them."

"And Christ never condemned anyone," Mrs. McCarthy told him, as intense now as he was.

"Well, you'll have to choose between your politics and your religion. All I can say is if you don't agree with the Church's teaching, then you have no place in this chapel."

It was his parting shot and with it he knew he had bested her. She looked at him for a long minute in silence so that he blushed again, thinking for a moment that she was going to chide him, maternally perhaps, for being cheeky to his elders. But she didn't. Instead she shook her elbow free of his hand and walked slowly away from him out of the chapel. He stood, until he had recovered his composure, then he too walked outside. To his relief she was nowhere to be seen.

When Mrs. McCarthy returned home her son, Harry, knew something was wrong, and when she told him what had happened he was furious. She had to beg him not to go up to the chapel there and then.

"He said what, Ma? Tell me again!"

She started to recount her story.

"No, not that bit. I'm not concerned about all that. It's the end bit I can't take in. The last thing he said to you. Tell me that again?"

"He said if I didn't agree then I had no place in the chapel," she told him again, almost timidly.

"The ignorant-good-for-nothing wee skitter," Harry fumed, pacing the floor. Mrs. McCarthy was sorry she had told him anything. "I'll have to learn to bite my tongue," she told herself. "If I'd said nothing to the priest none of this would have happened." Harry's voice burst in on her thoughts.

"What gets me is that you reared nine of us. That's what gets me! You did your duty as a Catholic mother and that's the thanks you get for it. They've no humility, no sense of humanity. Could he not see that you're an old woman."

"That's nothing to do with it," Mrs. McCarthy interrupted him sharply.

"Ma, that's everything to do with it! Can you not see that? If he had been talking to me I could see the point, but you? All your life you've done your best and he insults you like that! He must have no mother of his own. That's all they're good for: laying down their petty little rules and lifting their collections and insulting the very people. . ."

"Harry, that's enough."

The weariness in her tone stopped him in mid-sentence.

"I've had enough arguing to do me for one day," she said. "You giving off like that is doing me no good. Just forget about it for now. And I don't want you doing anything about it; I'll see Fr. Burns again in my own good time. But for now, I'm not going to let it annoy me any more."

But it did. It ate away at her all day and when she retired to bed it was to spend a restless night with Fr. Burns's words turning over again and again in her mind.

Choose between your politics and your religion. Politics and religion. If you don't accept the Church's teachings you've no place in the chapel. No place in the chapel.

The next day she went to chapel as was her custom but she didn't go at her usual time and she was nervous and unsettled within herself all the time she was there. Even Our Lady couldn't settle her. She was so worried that Fr. Burns would arrive and that they would have another row that she couldn't concentrate on her prayers. Eventually it became too much for her and she left by the side door and made her way home again, agitated and in bad form.

The next few days were the same. She made her way to the chapel as usual but she did so in an almost furtive manner and the solace that she usually got from her daily prayers and contemplation was lost to her. On the Wednesday she walked despondently to the shops; on her way homewards she bumped into Jinny Blake outside McErlean's Home Bakery.

"Ach, Mrs. McCarthy, how'ye doing? You look as if everybody belonging t'ye had just died. What ails ye?"

Mrs. McCarthy told her what had happened, glad to get talking to someone who, unlike Harry or Fr. Burns, would understand her dilemma. Jinny was a sympathetic listener and she waited attentively until Mrs. McCarthy had furnished her with every detail of the encounter with the young priest.

"So that's my tale of woe, Jinny," she concluded eventually, "and I don't know what to do. I'm not as young as I used to be. . ."

"You're not fit for all that annoyance. The cheek of it!" her friend reassured her. "You shouldn't have to put up with the like of that at your age. You seldom hear them giving off about them ones."

Jinny gestured angrily at a passing convoy of British Army Landrovers.

"They bloody well get off too light, God forgive me and pardon me! Imagine saying that to you, or anyone else for that matter."

Jinny was angry but whereas Harry's rage had unsettled Mrs. McCarthy Jinny's indignation fortified her, so that by the time they finally parted Mrs. McCarthy was resolved to confront Fr. Burns and, as Jinny had put it, to "stand up for her rights."

The following afternoon she made her way to the chapel. It was her intention to go from there to the Parochial House. She was quite settled in her mind as to what she would say and how she would say it but first she knelt before the statue of Our Lady. For the first time that week she felt at ease in the chapel. But the sound of footsteps coming down the aisle in her direction unnerved her slightly. She couldn't look around to see who it was, which made her even more anxious that it might be Fr. Burns. In her plans the confrontation with him was to be on her terms in the Parochial House, not here, on his terms, in the chapel.

"Hullo, Mrs. McCarthy, is that you?" With a sigh of relief she recognized Fr. Kelly's voice.

"Ah, Father," she exclaimed. "It is indeed. Am I glad to see you!"

Fr. Kelly was the parish priest. He was a small, stocky, white-haired man in his late fifties. He and Mrs. McCarthy had known each other since he had taken over the parish fifteen years before. As he stood smiling at her, obviously delighted at her welcome for him, she reproached herself for not coming to see him long before this. As she would tell Jinny later, that just went to show how distracted she was by the whole affair.

"Fr. Kelly, I'd love a wee word with you, so I would," she rose slowly from her pew. "If you have the time, that is."

"I've always time for you, my dear."

He helped her to her feet.

"Come on and we'll sit ourselves down over here."

They made their way to a secluded row of seats at the side of the church. Fr. Kelly sat quietly as Mrs. McCarthy recounted the story of her disagreement with Fr. Burns. When she was finished he remained silent for some moments, gazing quizzically over at the altar.

"Give up your politics or give up your religion, Mrs. McCarthy? That's the quandary, isn't it?"

He spoke so quietly, for a minute she thought he was talking to himself. Then he straightened up in the seat, gave her a smile and asked, "Are you going to give up your politics?"

"No," she replied a little nervously and then, more resolutely: "No! Not even for the Pope of Rome."

He nodded in smiling assent and continued, "And are you going to give up your religion?"

"No," she responded quickly, a little surprised at his question.

"Not even for the Pope of Rome?" he bantered her.

"No," she smiled, catching his mood.

"Well then, I don't know what you're worrying about. We live in troubled times and it's not easy for any of us, including priests. We all have to make our own choices. That's why God gives us the power to reason and our own free will. You've heard the Church's teaching and you've made your decision. You're not going to give up your religion nor your politics and I don't see why you should. All these other things will pass. And don't bother yourself about seeing Fr. Burns. I'll have a wee word with him."

He patted her gently on the back of her hand as he got to his feet.

"Don't be worrying. And don't let anyone put you out of the chapel! It's God's house. Hold on to all your beliefs, Mrs. McCarthy, if you're sure that's what you want."

"Thank you, Father." Mrs. McCarthy smiled in relief. "God bless you."

"I hope He does," Fr. Kelly said, "I hope He does." He turned and walked slowly up the aisle. When he got to the door he turned and looked down the chapel. Mrs. McCarthy was back at her favorite seat beside the statue of Our Lady. Apart from her the silent church was empty. Fr. Kelly stood reflecting pensively on that. For a moment he was absorbed by the irony of the imagery before him. Then he turned wearily, smiled to himself, and left.

Just a Game

SAINT PATRICK'S under-14 hurling team possessed three mentors. All had been accomplished hurlers in their own time and, like most sportsmen and old soldiers, they refused to die. Indeed, they refused even to fade away, and with a zeal which was as strong as it had been in their youth they had successfully steered the Under-14s through club honors, and now their charges were poised to represent the county at the All-Ireland *Féile* tournament.

Mickey MacAteer, the team manager, was assisted by Leo Murphy and "wee" Eoin Rafferty. Leo was a Dubliner and although he had never lost his love for that fair city, Ballymurphy, where he taught at the local school, had been his home for the last ten years. Wee Eoin and Mickey were both Falls Road men, unemployed building laborers who lived in Ballymurphy.

The lads in the Under-14 panel combined urban toughness (a quality for which Saint Patrick's was renowned at all levels) with a fast, close style of hurling. They became the County Antrim *Féile* champions after a tough campaign, especially against clubs from the rural north of the county. Their rivals never gave an inch and every game was a hard-fought contest. Parochial and other ancient rivalries played their parts and verbal abuse from the sidelines was commonplace; during one game youthful supporters of a team from the Glens even began to chant: "They eat dogs in Ballymurphy." The older Saint Pat's members and spectators were affronted by such a smear tactic—especially the mothers present, who, mortified by the insult, replied with suitably descriptive disclaimers. The youngsters seemed not to care and went on to win the match. Later, when presented with the trophy the day they won the county final, Big Charlie the team captain delighted his teammates and made their euphoric mentors wince when he exclaimed: "Up the Dog Eaters! *Tiocfaidh ár lá!*".*

The delight of the young players was infectious and that night Charlie's acceptance speech raised a laugh among the adults in the bar at Saint Pat's as they celebrated the junior team's victory. It was a great night. None of the winning team were there, of course, as they were all under age, but Mickey, wee Eoin and Leo were their very capable, committed and experienced representatives. They knew exactly how to handle such an occasion: they got drunk.

The weeks after that were spent training for the national finals of the *Féile*. Three evenings each week the team got together after school and wee Eoin put them through their paces again and again and again. At weekends Saint Pat's Under-16 team or the Minors gave them a practice game. The mentors were on hand throughout: they threatened, bullied, encouraged and begged their team into shape, and in between they discussed tactics and the ins-and-outs of different players playing in different positions. For some of the boys it was a worrying time. They had a panel of twenty and everyone was eager to win a place on the team. Some, like Big Burger, Charlie, Seamus, Patrick and Packy, Seanie and Jimmy were assured of their places. They were the core of the team but the rest of the places were open to whoever was on form. For this reason there was a consistently full turnout at all the training sessions.

---

* Our day will come

This involvement in the preparations wasn't confined to the team and its trainers, or even to the Under-16 or Minor players. The entire club campaigned to take the All-Ireland *Féile* trophy and bring it over the border and into the North, and more importantly into Saint Patrick's in Ballymurphy. So it was that when the *Féile* weekend arrived two buses of supporters and the team, all bedecked in the club and county colors, gathered to make the journey to Kildare, and they left the club grounds to the cheers and best wishes of their clubmates and parents.

"That's it," Mickey said. "We're off."

And so they were. The drive down to the border was uneventful. They were stopped for a few minutes at the huge British Army checkpoint outside Newry and after that the journey to Dublin passed quickly. Many of the boys had never been so far across the border before, though most of them had been on sponsored holidays in Belgium and further afield. They stopped for a noisy meal in Swords and then in Dublin and the boys and their mentors spent an hour in O'Connell Street wandering between the GPO and an amusement arcade. It was late in the afternoon by the time they finally pulled into Naas. The boys were staying in the homes of members of a local club, and a representative met the bus and gave Mickey the accommodation arrangements for the weekend. He also gave him a list of fixtures. Mickey read through the list.

"Look at this," he turned to Leo and wee Eoin, thrusting the *Féile* program under their noses. "We've been drawn to play against a local club tonight. Bloody chancers! They're trying to make sure their team has the advantage. It's not right. They're playing on their own pitch and we've come all the way from Belfast; our lads are bound to be tired after the journey. They should have put all the ones that have to travel together. That way it would have been fair. I'm going to complain!"

He did so but to no avail, and by the time the Saint Pat's lads were in the dressing room an hour or so later, togged out and ready for their first encounter, Mickey was in a foul mood.

Leo and Eoin had finished their team talk. It was only a minute or so before the throw-in. Mickey, as befitted his status as manager, always had the last word. He looked around at the eager, anxious young faces gazing up at him.

"Right, boys. This is what we've all worked for. Yous know the score. Yous are good. Yous are the best in County Antrim. But we're not in County Antrim now. We're in the Free State. They must have heard how good yous are 'cos they've drawn us against the local team. The referee's probably local also. They're all well rested and we're only after a long journey, but you know what? We can still beat them and that's what we're going to do. We're going to go out there and teach these uns how to play hurley."

He looked around his team.

"Right?" he snapped at them.

"Right!"

"Right?" Mickey and Leo and wee Eoin shouted in chorus.

"Right!" the boys clamored, banging their hurleys and their studded boots on the floor.

"Well get out there and do it!" Mickey growled.

And so they did. It wasn't a hard game but even when it was clear that they were the superior team Saint Pat's took no chances. They played at full stretch right up to the final whistle and finished twelve points ahead of the devastated opposition. In the dressing room afterwards the lads were jubilant. Mickey congratulated them, but he was grudging in his praise.

"All right, yous did well. But that's only what we expected. Tonight was aisy. Wee buns! It wasn't a real test for yous. That comes the morra. We have two games. That's if yous play better than tonight. The third game's the semi-final but you have to beat two good teams to get there. So tonight I want yous all in bed early and back here in the morning at ten for a team talk. Okay?"

Within half an hour all the boys were piled into cars which distributed them to houses throughout the neighborhood. There the "young lads from Belfast" were plied with good food and sympathetic questions about how they and their families were able to manage at home with "the troubles." For the first time some of the boys saw the daily happenings of their native city through the eyes of sympathetic spectators, and for the first time some of them wondered how indeed they and their families managed. As they slipped off to sleep they felt flattered that they did.

The three mentors had a similar experience over a meal and later a few pints as guests of the local club, but they kept the storytelling about the troubles to a minimum. Unlike their young players, they were naturally and instinctively cautious about declaring their political views to strangers and, although all three would probably have agreed generally on political matters, there were issues that Mickey and Eoin had never really discussed with Leo, and a pub in County Kildare wasn't the place to start. Apart from all that, as Mickey observed only half jokingly, they had a *Féile* tournament to win and needed to return early to their boardinghouse to plan the next day's team tactics.

By late afternoon on the following day it was obvious that these tactics were the right ones. The morning match against Louth was tough but Saint Pat's won through in the end. They were victorious also in their second game, against Kilkenny.

It was the same story early on Sunday morning at the semi-final. The Saint Pat's supporters were nursing hangovers after a late-night session but were rewarded for their early morning sacrifices with a narrow, hard-won victory over Limerick. By now the Ballymurphy lads had won a sizable following from supporters of the other counties. They and the Belfast contingent were ecstatic. Mickey, Leo and wee Eoin were overjoyed also, but their main concern now was to rest the team. It had been a hard weekend and the hardest part was still to come. They shepherded the boys off the pitch and into the bus.

"We're going off somewhere for something light to eat after yous get a shower. We're all staying together until the game," Mickey told them.

The match was at half-three but first there was open-air mass in the grounds of a local college and a parade from there along a route of a few hundred yards to the college pitch for the final. The parade was to be led by the finalists, so while the boys showered Leo sorted out the parade arrangements and loaded a clean set of jerseys onto the bus. They spent the next few hours at a small hotel about ten miles outside the town. Every one of them was nervous, but as time passed there was a collective settling of tension and Mickey entertained them with stories, with punchlines which told mostly against himself. They talked about everything except the match until finally the time came for the team to tog out in their clean strips. Packy and Seamus were selected to carry the club banner. Before they boarded the bus again, a little subdued this time, Mickey, Leo and wee Eoin offered their last few words of encouragement. Mickey, as was the custom, had the last word.

"Yous know yous can win this match. I'm not going to talk too much about that. Yous are tired but so's the other team. I only want to say that win or lose yous have done us all proud."

He looked around at the boys.

"Yous are the best squad I've ever coached, so just go out there and do your best and the three of us'll be happy."

Mickey's team talks were usually fairly long so this brevity caught everyone by surprise and for a minute after he had finished the entire group stood in silence. It was Big Charlie who broke the spell by grasping and shaking Mickey's hand. Then as each boy boarded the bus Leo, Mickey and wee Eoin embraced or shook hands with them. For years afterwards everyone who was there said that the few hours at the hotel was a special experience. After that the waiting seemed unbearably long and even the honor of leading the parade seemed of less significance.

The parade itself was a colorful affair. There were about twenty-five teams resplendent in their colors and headed by their club banners, and about 2,000 local and visiting spectators and half a dozen bands. The President of Ireland was there waiting on the back of a huge covered lorry which had been transformed into an altar and a reviewing stand. Wee Eoin counted five bishops, each bedecked in purple robes. Before the mass started the President came down off the lorry to inspect an honor guard of soldiers in ceremonial uniform while the *Garda* band played martial airs. The Saint Patrick's supporters were greatly impressed by the pomp and ceremony of the occasion. Old Jimmy Conlon from Andersonstown, whose grandson was a Saint Pat's sub, was moved to tears as he turned to wee Eoin and whispered, "It's great to be free, Eoin, isn't it?" Wee Eoin thought the scene was a bit like something out of Franco's Spain but he said nothing. There was no harm in old Jimmy and he would get endless satisfaction recounting the day to his cronies back in the club.

Eoin was only happy when he, Mickey and Leo were finally in the dressing room with the team. The dressing rooms were contained in a single-storeyed pavilion-type structure made of concrete blocks. The room allocated to Saint Pat's was divided from their opponents' quarters by a movable partition which was pulled across in sections on rollers on the floor and ceiling.

The boys were ready for action. They stood in a semi-circle around Leo, who repeated once again the instructions for play. Earlier he had watched their opponents playing; now he passed on the intelligence he had gathered, giving each of the players specific instructions for the match. When Leo was finished Eoin said his few words and Mickey concluded the briefing.

"This Waterford team is good but yous are better. Remember that. They can't beat yous. Yous might be nervous of them. That's all right. That's natural. But don't forget they're even more nervous of yous. And yous know why! 'Cos yous are from the North. Nothing can beat yous. So get out there, get settled as quickly as possible and play hurley!"

The Waterford team was good. Within five minutes the Saint Pat's lads knew they were in trouble. The Waterford squad, with a few exceptions, were bigger than them and they played to suit their height, a fast, mobile, hand-passing, high-fielding game. Saint Pat's never gave an inch, but for all their efforts Waterford scored a goal after about twenty minutes. From then on the Waterford forwards hunted in packs so that for most of the remainder of the first half the *sliotar** was rarely out of their possession. Had it not been for the dogged determination of the Saint Patrick's back line the score would

---

* hurling ball

have been in cricket figures. As it was, the half-time scoreboard read Waterford one goal and two points to Antrim nil.

Mickey, Leo and wee Eoin had spent the first half roaming endlessly up and down the sideline shouting and coaxing, cajoling and cursing. Now as they walked off the pitch to join the youngsters in the dressing room they knew what was wrong. Their team was knackered. They had played their hearts out to get to the final and now they had nothing else to give. When the men reached the dressing room they were met with a depressed silence. The boys sat dejectedly on the benches, while from the Waterford side of the partition came a happy hum of noise and a buzz of laughter and high spirits.

"Come on lads, let's be having yous," Leo began. "Heads up, come on."

Seamus was lying on his back. As he obediently and automatically sat up Mickey saw the tearmarks on his cheeks.

"Jesus, boys!" Leo exploded, "It's only a bloody game. It's not the end of the world."

The rest of the boys pulled themselves dispiritedly into sitting positions but even then their attention was elsewhere. Beyond the partition there was an outburst of loud clapping and chanting: "Waterford, Waterford, Waterford!" followed by a low murmur of talk.

Wee Eoin went to the partition and put his eye to the gap between one of the joints. The Waterford team were sitting upright and alert, hurling sticks in hand as they listened to their manager. He was addressing them in a low, intense staccato, emphasizing his instructions by jabbing his finger in the air. Eoin couldn't hear what he was saying but as he watched there was another outburst of chanting and laughing. He turned to face his own team.

Mickey was looking at him. He had a little smile on his face. "What's that they're saying next door, Eoin?" he asked.

Eoin looked at him, puzzled.

"I thought I heard them say something about Belfast dickheads," Mickey continued.

"Oh aye," Eoin agreed. "They're in quare form. They think we're a crowd of tubes. Wait till I hear what your man's saying now."

Some of the boys looked up as he put his ear to the gap in the partition.

"Shit!" Eoin hissed.

"What was that?" Mickey asked.

"Nawh," Eoin replied, "I'll tell you later."

The entire team looked up at him expectantly.

"Tell us what they're saying," Mickey commanded. "The boys deserve to know."

"He's saying that the game's over. It's in the bag. All the talk about teams from the North is spoof, especially Belfast. They're talking about whitewashing us."

Mickey eyed his squad.

"Is that right, Charlie? Eh? What about you, Seamus? And Gearóid? Have yous lost your tongues? C'mon, Jimmy? Seamus?"

His interrogation was interrupted by a loud burst of applause from across the partition.

"Some boy made a crack about Yella Murphy," Eoin told them.

Mickey reached over and grabbed Big Charlie's hurley. He rattled it on the bench. His tone was urgent as he spoke.

"That's it lads. Where are yous from? Ballymurphy, Ballymurphy, Ballymurphy!" he chanted.

The din in the Waterford quarters intensified in retaliation. Big Charlie grabbed his stick back. He joined in Mickey's war chant, rattling his studded boots on the floor and beating his hurley on the bench. The rest of the team joined him so that from each side of the partition the noise rose to a crescendo. As they yelled and bawled and drummed out their defiance the Saint Pat's mood changed completely. When Mickey began to speak again they quietened immediately and listened eagerly to his instructions.

"Now boys, we're going to change tactics. They want to play their brand of hurling: we're going to stop them! We're going to harass and spoil and harry and block. They want us to play their game. We can't; we're too tired. So don't try any fancy stuff; let the ball do the running. Don't play across the field or waste energy with short passes; play long balls up and down the wings. Backs!"

He addressed the backs.

"Stick to your men like glue, like their shadows—only closer! Get inside them. Get your sticks up and get to every ball first and hit it first time. Don't even try to lift it, just get it away down the wings into their half! And no fouling. We can't afford to give away any frees."

The boys nodded in unison.

"Forwards keep moving. Spread their defenses. The midfield will feed you the ball. Take your points. No fancy stuff! Just steady sniping over the bar. Don't try to run in or they'll destroy yous. Get the ball; look up; get it over the crossbar. That's it! Can yous do that?"

"Yes," they nodded determinedly, and now they were on their feet, hurleys in hand, tiredness and sore limbs forgotten. Across the partition all was quiet. Their opponents were already out on the pitch.

Mickey faced them again but it was Leo who spoke, his Dublin twang thicker than ever with the emotion.

"Where are we from?" he shouted.

"From Dirty Dublin," wee Eoin laughed.

"From Ballybleedingmurphy," Leo corrected him.

"From where?" he challenged the team.

"From Ballybleedingmurphy," they mimicked.

"And yous can't be beaten," Mickey reminded them.

The next thirty-five minutes saw the most exciting and courageous exhibition of close-quarter hurling that most of the spectators had seen or ever would see again. The Waterford team were thwarted at every turn but they kept their nerve, so that the play surged back and forth without a score for the first twenty minutes. Then Jimmy sent a long high shot in towards the Waterford goalmouth. It struck the upright and bounced back into play just outside the square. As the Waterford fullback moved to clear it wee Packie was in before him and on to the ball like a cat on a mouse. He never even broke his stride as he sent the *sliotar* rocketing into the back of the net.

The spectators went wild. Wee Packy was like a banty cock as he strutted about, shouting his team on. The Waterford goalie and the fullback were arguing.

"Where did he come from?" the Waterford fullback exclaimed. Packie looked up at him.

"I came from Ballymurphy," he snarled. "We eat dogs!"

That score was quickly followed by a point and then another one so that with only minutes to go the teams were level. Mickey was like a dervish on the sideline; Leo had lost his voice. Wee Eoin was up behind the goals willing dangerous balls away. Then at midfield Big Charlie picked up a loose ball and passed it to wee Gerry McKeown. Gerry stopped, looked up and sent a perfect long puck over the crossbar to put Saint Patrick's and Antrim into the lead.

Bedlam reigned. The referee looked at his watch. A chorus of whistles rang out from the Belfast spectators. But play continued, and then, seconds later, just in the dying minute of the game Waterford made another valiant, desperate surge towards the Saint Patrick's goal. A low shot was miraculously saved on the line by Gary the Saint Pat's keeper; there was a frenzied scramble for the *sliotar* as it bounced out from the goal. A Waterford player got to it first but was robbed almost immediately by Gary who had followed the ball out. As he moved to clear his lines for the second time, while wee Eoin screamed from behind the posts, "Help him, help him, somebody help him!" his shot was expertly blocked down.

The loose ball bounced back towards the goal and dribbled slowly—almost in slow motion—into the back of the net. For a split second there was silence. Then as the ball settled in the dust the long piercing scream of the final whistle brought the game to an end.

Mickey embraced each of the exhausted youngsters as they came off the field to the cheers of the spectators still ringing from the sidelines. Big Charlie began to sob when Mickey grabbed him. He shook himself free and stood facing the three team mentors. He was covered in sweat, smeared with mud and his hair was plastered to his forehead. His hurling stick jutted defiantly from his clenched fist.

"They won," he blubbered, "but they never beat us."

Mickey grabbed him again. Leo and wee Eoin patted them both on the back.

"They'll never beat yous, son," Leo said. "Never."

A Safe Bet

I N THE AFTERNOON of the day, and particularly on a Saturday, in most towns in most parts of Ireland a procession of people can be seen making their hurried way back and forth between public house and bookmaker's shop. For all I know this pedestrian perambulation, or a variation of it, may occur also in foreign parts. I make no claims in this regard. Indeed, if I am honest—and, of course, like most people, even if I wasn't I would pretend that I was—I would have to admit that my experience of this ritual to-ing and fro-ing betwixt pub and bookies is confined to Belfast town. Nitpicking readers may therefore wish to challenge the empirical evidence of my opening sentence.

Let them do so if they must. I am undismayed by such pettiness, especially because I know that the more discerning reader like yourself will have no time for such distracting trifles. And anyway, do we have to provide scientific research or documentary proof to support everything we say? Of course not; not unless we are totally lacking in imagination. And that not being the case, neither you nor I need worry. Meanwhile, in their never-ending scurrying after facts the mindless drones will never read stories such as this. They are lost to the real world and beyond temptation or redemption. They will certainly never be found in that jostling, animated, nervous, hopeful, optimistic collection of humanity which spends its Saturday afternoons and, depending on individual circumstances, the afternoons of other days, rushing back and forth between public house and bookmaker's shop in Belfast, and—dare I say it?—most towns in most parts of Ireland.

Belfast is not much different from Derry or Dublin or Cork or Waterford or Limerick. These cities also have their optimists, their sporting gentlemen, their lovers of life, so I include them all in that great fraternity which is the main subject of our story. You may have noticed that I use the term sporting gentlemen. Lest the more feminist among you jump to conclusions, let me reassure you: this is no sexist slip. No! I am as liberated as any Irish mother's son can be. I am also zealously aware of the pitfalls of stereotyping. I know, too, how deeply sexist a language the English language is. I choose my words carefully and make no apologies for my use of the masculine noun. The term gentlemen instead of gentlepersons or gentle people or even gentlemen and gentlewomen is employed because the female sex is hardly ever, and in my experience never represented in the mobile, male and motley multitude of public-house punters which it is my intention to tell you about, eventually.

This is not to say that women don't drink. That would be unthinkable. Or that they don't gamble! Of course they do! Well, at least some of them do, and as you are no doubt aware and hopefully in favor of, these days some females are also seen in public bars, though not as frequently as the male of the species and never, as I have remarked above, as part of the mobile gambling clientele. Women, I suppose, in many ways are much too sensible for that. Or maybe, I hear you mutter under your breath, maybe they simply don't have the time?

Or maybe it's just the way we are. I mean, can you recall, even among the drinking and gambling women of your acquaintance, any who spent all their Saturdays between the bookies and the pub?

Can you think of the last time a mother or wife pulled on her coat on a Saturday afternoon and informed her family and partner that she was away off for a few pints and a wee bet? Or do you know any husband who answers a query about his wife's whereabouts with the cheerful information, as he tidies the house, does the shopping and prepares the dinner, that she's only away out with her mates for a few jars and a wager? No, of course you don't; such men don't exist. Not yet. And not in Belfast. Which is why, more than any other reason, I suppose, that the traffic 'twixt pub and bookies is so completely male-dominated.

Some of the more naïve among you may think that money is the cause of this imbalance. You may think that money, or more specifically the lack of it, may be a big problem for many women. This could well be true. Money, or more specifically the lack of it, is a problem for most of us and as women in Ireland are the most of us I'm sure it's a big problem for the most of them also.

Be that as it may, let me say without fear of contradiction—and there may well be some begrudgers among you who will say I have sufficient experience not to be contradicted—a lack of cash is never an insurmountable problem for the man who wants a drink. Thus it is that without a penny to his name a Belfast male can cheerfully contemplate an afternoon of *craic* and diversion. He requires only a few cronies and a Belfast location or alternatively a few Belfast cronies and any location, provided prohibition isn't the order of the day. Prohibition, as you probably know, isn't on order day or night in Belfast. Unemployment is, though. So it is that some Belfast males have plenty of time and little money. It's a safe bet that these are the main men, in Belfast or anywhere else for that matter, plying their optimists' trade in the bookies. It is also a non-sectarian, secular occupation, undisturbed by our current constitutional crisis and practiced on the Shankill as diligently as it is on the Falls.

Take last Saturday for example. If you were walking down the Falls Road and were not too preoccupied with your own concerns you may have noticed a small, pleasant-faced man standing at the Rock Bar. If you were really interested you may have noted that he arrived there at twelve noon. It was a fine morning and as our friend stood on the sidewalk he was greeted in a friendly manner by most of the people who passed by. Indeed, if you passed by yourself, you too may have exchanged a few words of cheerful salutation. Such is the feeling of bonhomie exuded by our friend.

After about half an hour he was joined by another man. If you were still watching, and provided you were not a stranger and not therefore by this time the subject, yourself, of surveillance by the local citizenry, you would have deduced from their manner of greeting one another that the two men were meeting by appointment. The first man is called Tucker McKnight; the second is Sean McCrory. Not that it matters. They could be any of us; they could even be you or me.

You may also have deduced that they had no money. Why otherwise would they meet outside and not inside the Rock Bar? Of all the possible reasons the lack of cash seems the most likely one. It is also the correct one, as the conversation of our two friends bears out.

"You're late! What kept y'?"

"I was trying to pick out a few winners and I didn't see the time going."

"You didn't get that few bob you were hoping for?"

"Nawh, what about yourself? Did the wife come across?"

"Nawh."

"Dead on."

"What d' y' say?"

"I said, dead on."

"Aye."

At this point the first man turned his pleasant smile once again on the passersby while his colleague fished a newspaper from his coat pocket and proceeded to study the form on the racing page. Every few minutes or so he would seek the advice of his mate and when that was cheerfully given he would return to his perusal of the day's race-meetings. After ten or perhaps fifteen minutes of this leisurely activity a number of men came out of the pub, passed Sean and Tucker and proceeded a few paces up the road to Graham's Bookmakers. On their return a few minutes later they were questioned by our two heroes.

"What won the first one at Epsom?"

"Little Lady at two to one."

"I knew that!" Sean exclaimed.

"What do you fancy in the 1:15 at Newbury?" one of the men asked.

"Nordic Flash," Tucker suggested. "It's a safe bet and it's seven to one."

"D'ye reckon?" the man replied. "I fancied Natural Ability."

"No chance," Sean scoffed. "Tucker's right. Nordic Flash is a sure thing."

"Maybe you're right," the man mused. Thoughtfully, he retraced his steps to the bookies. Tucker smiled at his retreating back.

"There goes our savior," he said.

"I hope you're right," said Sean.

"Of course I am. Did I ever put you on a bum steer? If Nordic Flash comes in like you say it will, me and you is on the pig's back."

And so they were. Nordic Flash didn't let them down. The man who sought their advice put a fiver on it and on his way back to the bar he presented Sean with the five-pound note.

"There y'are," he said, "that'll get yous a drink."

"Good man yourself," they saluted him.

By now they had been joined by a third party. His name was Big Mickey Nelson, or Bonaparte to his friends.

"What about yis?"

"Dead on. And yourself? What about you?"

"Grand. D'yis fancy a pint?"

"Are you breaking into your Holy Communion money, or what?"

"Nawh, you got that off me at the time. I tapped the wife for a few bob out of her club money. This is her good week. So when I saw the two of yous standing here like two hoors at a hockey match I thought I'd treat yous. Now, do yous want a pint or not? I need a cure, so if yous are coming yous better come now!"

"Well, if you put it like that we'll not see you stuck, will we Tucker?"

"Indeed and we will not, Sean."

And with that the three of them went into the Rock, which just proves that my Aunt Maggie is right when she says that there's them that'll give you a pint quicker than a loaf for your table. She's right, but that's not really the point I suppose. Our two friends never asked for anything. It was offered to them. That's not to say that there aren't those who do ask; of course there are. And I'm not talking about the crass coat-tuggers or common-or-garden tappers, though they too have their place in the scheme of things. Some, indeed, are quite famous, as are their haunts, but we'll make no judgment on that; such men are to be admired for their tenacity. No, I'm thinking here of the finer exponents of the art. Veterans like Tedbert or An Fear Gorm, the Blue Man, but they rarely enter bookmakers' premises and are different therefore from Sean or Tucker who represent more fully the subject of this thesis. Our subjects are almost casual manifestations of an aspect of our social culture: Tedbert and An Fear Gorm represent something more. They are in many ways like the old professional saloon-bar gambler. A breed apart, they live for the challenge of winning against the odds. I know one such, wee Paddy Bartley, who went out one Saturday at four o'clock with only £1 in his pocket and came home stocious at midnight with a sixpack of Guinness, a half bottle of Vodka for Liz, his ever-loving and patient partner, forty Park Drive, crisps for the kids, a Chinese carry-out and £5.53 cash. He never bothered declaring the money to Liz. Fair is fair, and anyway, it's all he had left after buying the last two rounds. That man was a master of his art. That's high-flying whiz-kiddery. Here we're dealing with more ordinary matters.

Back at the Rock Bar our less ambitious amigos were sipping tentatively on their pints. Napoleon was in the toilet. He found it difficult to go there or to return without somebody asking if he had met his Waterloo. It was a standing joke in the Rock, but Napoleon wasn't amused; today was no different.

"Friggin' smart Alecs," he grumbled as he elbowed his way in beside Sean and Tucker.

"I think we'll put a few bob on Miss Musky," Sean suggested.

"What about 50p each way and we can get a bottle of stout each and watch it on TV?"

"No problem," Tucker and Napoleon agreed.

The three of them joined the little throng which was exiting hurriedly at that minute from the bar and made their way to the bookies. Sean walked up to the counter.

"Hold on!" Tucker halted him.

"Make it a £2 double on Miss Musky and Sweet Prince. I think this'll be our lucky day."

"Are you sure?"

"The going at Doncaster suits Sweet Prince. He's favorite. If Miss Musky comes in that'll be fourteen quid riding on a two-to-one favorite. It's a safe bet. What do you say, Napoleon?"

"No problem."

"Okay," Sean agreed.

He passed the extra money across to the clerk and placed his bet. The trio made their hopeful way back to the Rock. Inside they watched Miss Musky romp home; Sweet Prince was beaten in a photo-finish. Sean crumpled the beaten docket in his hand and cast it among its fellows on the barroom floor. There were no recriminations.

Twenty minutes later the three of them were back outside the bar. It was a pleasant afternoon and as they stood there they were greeted in a friendly manner by most of the people who passed by. Indeed, if you passed by yourself, you too may have exchanged a few words of cheerful salutation. Such was the aura of bonhomie exuded by them. Napoleon was enjoying the sun and engaging in occasional banter with the perpetual posse of punters who continued to trek between the pub and the bookies. Sean had fished his paper from his pocket once more and was studying the form intently. Every so often he would seek Tucker's advice and when that was cheerfully given he would return to his perusal of the evening's race-meetings. After ten or perhaps fifteen minutes of this leisurely activity they were joined by a man who detached himself from the slipstream of the crowd toing and fro-ing on the pavement.

"What do yous fancy for the big race?" he asked.

They all looked at Sean.

"Red Horizon," he said.

"I agree," Tucker nodded.

"Maybe you're right," the man mused. He retraced his steps thoughtfully. Tucker smiled widely at his retreating back.

"There goes our savior," he said.

"I hope you're right," said Sean.

"Yous owe me a pint," said Napoleon.

"Do y' hear him?" Tucker grinned.

"No problem," Sean said confidently to Napoleon. "Did we ever let you down? It's early days yet. You'll get your pint."

"I'm only slagging," said Napoleon.

"I know," said Tucker.

"It's a sure thing," Sean beamed. "A safe bet."

That's the way it is in the afternoons of most days, and particularly on Saturdays, in most towns in most parts of Ireland. Sean and Tucker, and Napoleon too of course, though he may deny it, are part of a great tradition. Like many traditions it and they may die out, though I doubt it. They are life's great optimists. They have a vision far beyond their present status which sustains them through all life's difficulties. They could be overtaken by modern trends; these things happen despite all our protestations. Women may even come to join the mobile mob, and in this regard my support for their involvement is now a matter of public record, and worth in the fullness of time a drink or two from the generous sex.

At any rate I have recorded the tradition as it now exists and before it is overtaken or replaced or amended. I do so for posterity. I trust that you, if you are not already numbered among the followers or exponents of this tradition, will now look with kinder eyes at the processions of punters you see making their hurried way back and forth between public house and bookmaker's shop. Cast a tolerant eye on them. For if they vanish we will never see the like of them again.

How Paddy McGlade Entered
Into a State of Grace

PADDY McGLADE WAS as good and kind and as thoughtful a soul as you would ever care to meet. He was a quiet, shy little man. That's when he was sober. He hadn't been sober in a good while. Well, that's not strictly true. He was frequently sober, but not for any significant period of time. Every few weeks he would be sober for a few days and once after he fell down the stairs to the lounge in Saint John's Gaelic Athletic Club, his few days lasted a full fortnight in hospital.

That was before he was saved. Now he doesn't drink at all. He is back home living with his mother and the two of them are as happy as can be. Well, Paddy is as happy as can be; his mother is just a lot happier than she used to be, and she won't be completely happy until Paddy is married. She is offering the big novena in Clonard that Paddy will meet a decent girl now that he is settled down and off the drink. Paddy's mother has great faith in the big novena in Clonard.

She swears by it. If you ask her she will tell you that that's what got Paddy off the drink, and maybe she's right.

Every June thousands of people crowd into the grounds of Clonard Monastery and the neighboring streets are jammed tight with cars from early morning till late at night. And the singing: you would hear it miles away up the Shankill or down the Falls, while the streets around the monastery are bedecked with blue-and-white bunting in honor of the Holy Mother. Local stewards also wear blue-and-white armbands, to distinguish them from impostors.

One year the Clonard novena almost caused an international incident when a British Army patrol intercepted a bunch of Clonard stewards directing traffic on the Springfield Road. It was during the Falklands war. Blue and white are Argentina's national colors and the squaddies thought they had stumbled across an Argentinean roadblock. The stewards didn't believe them. It took the intervention of the Clonard rector and a very senior British officer to sort things out, and eventually it was all resolved fairly amicably, though only just.

During the big novena at Clonard thousands and thousands of petitions are offered to Our Lady. The Redemptorist preachers read a sample of the petitions out at every novena: petitions for success in exams, for the safe return of a son, for a recovery from illness, for peace in Ireland, for a cure for alcoholism, for a baby, for the prisoners, for help with debt problems, for a decent house. Paddy McGlade's mother's petition was read out one day. The preacher, Fr. Browne, made special mention of it. "That my son may return to a state of grace, and for the happy repose of his father and for all the holy souls in purgatory: from a mother."

When Paddy's mother heard Fr. Browne reading that her heart leapt. She was sure that everyone knew that it was her petition, but of course they didn't. Still and all, between the shock of hearing her words read aloud and the wave of emotion which swept over her as the huge congregation prayed for her son to return to a state of grace, Paddy's mother knew that Our Lady was going to grant her petition.

That evening Paddy arrived at the Felons' Club slightly inebriated after a good day at the bookies. His first mistake was to complain noisily when the barman didn't serve him as quickly as Paddy thought he should. When the doorman arrived at the barman's request to escort him off the premises Paddy threw a punch at him. That was his second mistake. The Felons' is a very select establishment which prides itself on its quiet ambience and pleasant staff. Paddy's exit was swift and undignified. The manner of his going attracted a small crowd of passersby.

"You've shit in the nest now, me oul' son," one of them consoled Paddy, who was roaring his disapproval at the departing back of the doorman.

"You'd be better taking yourself off," another advised him.

"I suppose so," Paddy mumbled thickly. "They can stick their club!"

He crossed the road to Curley's supermarket, where his transaction at the off-license was more patient and successful. As he wandered back down the road again he had a bottle of Jameson's tucked snugly in a plastic bag in his coat pocket and a plan for the evening slowly fermenting in his head. He headed for the Sloan's Club and he resolved to cut across the Falls Park and up through the cemetery; it was shorter that way. By now it was also dark but this did not concern Paddy; not in the least. He leaned against a tree in the park and gazed down over the lights of Belfast. As he swigged at his bottle of whiskey his annoyance at the Felons' debacle was replaced with a feeling of quiet contentment. The enveloping dusk cloaked him in anonymity, soothing him as he made his way in the direction of the cemetery.

Others also make their way towards the cemetery. Indeed, much to the incomprehension and outrage of most respectable citizens, the city cemetery was habitually frequented by a host of nocturnal socialites. Most of them were harmless creatures, young people who couldn't afford to go to a bar or who wouldn't be served if they did. They gathered after dark to drink carry-outs of cheap lager or cider and play ghetto-blasters loudly. The cemetery was occasionally subjected to the destructive actions of an unrepresentative minority of vandals but the majority of cemetery users took no part in such actions. They drank their drink, annoyed or enjoyed each other and then left as they had entered, over the cemetery wall.

They weren't all teenagers. Joe Cooke, who went to the cemetery for an hour or so every night, was at least thirty. He and his dog Fred enjoyed the walk and if the night was fine they would sit and look down over the lights of the city and listen wistfully to its nighttime noises. The night that Paddy was making his way over the cemetery towards the Sloan's, as fate or Our Lady would have it, Joe Cooke and Fred were having one of their walks. Joe was drunk but Fred was sober.

Paddy sat down for a rest at the grave known as the Angel's grave. He didn't know that that was what it's called and he probably still doesn't. He just knew that he wanted to sit down and reflect on the state of the nation. Whiskey gets you like that. The first swig explores you inside and prepares the foundation for the second one. It warms the heart and belly and loosens the tongue. The second swig is meditative and relaxing. It encourages the third and permits a heady flow of witty repartee. After the fourth or fifth come songs of love and patriotism. Now, almost halfway down the bottle, comes the gift for wise and knowledgeable conversation on even the most difficult and intricate issues. That's the stage that Paddy was at as he seated himself at the Angel's grave.

The stages after that are always difficult to gauge. Some sing a song that everyone knows and joins in on. Others become sad or melancholy. Some cry. Others become romantic and believe themselves to be irresistibly sexy or funny, or both, at the same time. And others fight. In short, then, anything can happen.

Paddy seated himself at the edge of the grave. He held the whiskey bottle at arm's length in brief and silent contemplation before taking a long, greedy swig which propelled him beyond the state of uncertainty. He had been drinking since morning. It had been, he reflected, a long day. He was moved to look upwards at the stars and as he did so he keeled over backwards and fell, mouth towards the heavens. Here he lay snoring gently as Joe Cooke, unaware even of

Paddy's existence, made his slow, happy way towards his regular spot at the Angel's grave.

Joe was a big man, not so much in height as in bulk. Sometimes he didn't shave for a while and this seemed to add to his size. He had not one care in the whole world. He didn't even have a mother to worry him about her worrying about him. Sometimes this lack of a mother or any other relative willing to associate with him was a source of sorrow to Joe. Most times he was happy enough with Fred, but tonight was one of those times. He seated himself slowly at his usual spot with his back to the tombstone. He had a full bottle of original fine-quality cream sherry inside him and another half-bottle uncorked in his pocket. He started to sing.

> When the red red robin goes bob, bob bobbing
> along, . . . along,
> There'll be no more sighin' when he starts singing his old
> sweet song.
> Wake up, wake up you sleepy head, get up, wake up get out
> of bed,
> Live, love, laugh and be happy.

Joe sang in a deep bass but he didn't know one song the whole way through. His repertoire was limited. He stopped. Fred was missing. That in itself didn't worry Joe though it did surprise him, for while Fred went off on his own quite often he never left when Joe was singing, but sat at his feet and offered accompaniment.

Fred, however, was trying to waken Paddy. A big soft lump of a dog, when he found Paddy's sleeping form sprawled out on the grave behind Joe he just instinctively tried to lick him awake.

Joe, oblivious to all that was going on behind him, sipped at his sherry and contemplated the beauty of the starry sky. He wasn't a religious man but he did know the odd hymn from schooldays and he loved singing and, unlike songs, he knew hymns the whole way through.

> Sweet heart of Jesus
> Fount of love and mercy

120

To thee we call
Thy blessings to implore
O touch our hearts
So poor and so ungrateful.

Thus it was that Paddy started to come slowly back to life. The first sensation he felt was of warm breath and wet panting in his face. As he slowly opened his eyes the panting stopped. Paddy peered cautiously from his marble bed. He trembled a little with the cold. Overhead, he could see that the starry sky was partially blotted out by a huge white angel which towered above him. As Paddy stared in disbelief the angel started singing.

Sweet heart of Jesus we you implore
O make us love you more and more.

As he listened in petrified silence a strange wailing howl started up in harmony with the angel's voice.

Paddy slowly wet his trousers.

The angel spoke to him in a loud, good-humored voice. "Ah, I'm glad to see you, old friend. Where have you been? Why didn't you stay with me? You'll have to mend your ways, won't you? You've been a bad boy, a bad bad boy."

Paddy nodded his head slowly. The angel started to sing again.

Come Holy Ghost, Creator come,
Descend from heaven's throne.
Come take possession of our hearts,
And make them all your own.

Quietly, almost silently Paddy mouthed the words after him. As he did so he felt a sense of contentment envelope him. "Forgive me all my sins," he whispered.

It was at that moment, Paddy reckoned afterwards, that he entered into a state of grace. He was never to forget that exact minute, and years later as he decried the evils of drink Paddy could pinpoint the time of his conversion exactly.

Then, even as he savored the change coming over him, the strange howling started up again. The angel fell silent. Paddy seized his opportunity: he leapt to his feet and dashed off into the bushes, and as he made his frantic escape towards the wall he repeated over and over to himself a prayer his mother had taught him when he was a child.

"Jesus, Mary and Joseph, I give you my heart and my soul. Jesus, Mary and Joseph, assist us in our last agony. Jesus, Mary and Joseph, may we bring forth our souls in peace with you today."

Later that night, after a bath, a shave and a good feed he told his mother that he was taking the pledge.

"I knew you would," she said.

Paddy was humbled at her faith in him. In all his forty-six years she had never deserted him. Not once.

"I'm sorry, mother, for all the trouble I've caused you," he told her as tears of contrition trickled down his face. "I'll make it up to you," he promised. And so he did.

His mother told Paddy nothing of her petition, but she resolved to make a special thanksgiving to Our Lady at the next day's novena. She actually had to dissuade Paddy from going with her. Not that she didn't want him to go, but she didn't want anyone to realize that the petition Fr. Browne had read out that day had been for her Paddy.

Meanwhile, back at the Angel's grave Joe and Fred had been quite unperturbed by Paddy's flight from the cemetery. Fred had gone off to investigate the noise and had returned tugging a plastic bag with a three-quarters empty bottle of Jameson inside it. Joe sniffed the three or four inches of golden liquid tentatively.

"Aye, it's whiskey all right! Good boy."

He took an appreciative slug from the bottle.

"Ah, Fred; happy days. God is good. He works in wondrous ways."

Granny Harbinson

FROM HER SEAT at the window Granny Harbinson could see right up to the corner of Balaclava Street. She sat there always when Seamus was using the back room. "You can't be too careful," she'd tell him when the last of his friends had slipped in through the backyard.

"I don't want Minnie Clarke calling in when yous are here. Minnie's a terrible ould one for lettin' everybody know your business. She's nivver happy till she knows your whole history. She couldn't houl' her own water."

Seamus didn't use the house too often. Only when they were stuck for a place to meet. His granny embarrassed him with her conspiratorial ways when the boys were in, telling them to keep their voices down and turning the wireless up and then, sitting in the corner at the window, saying the rosary while they were in the back room. Her nerves were away with it, he thought, the way she carried on. Still, with all that, it was a good house and he was glad to sleep in it when the Brits were raiding up the road. His granny was sound enough.

He stayed after the meeting while she made him a cup of tea.

"Houl' on, son, and I'll run down to the corner for a bap for you. You can wait for a wee cup of tea in your hand, can't you?"

Seamus flung himself into the seat by the fire.

"Yes, Granny, I'm not going out till eight o'clock. I need the key," he added, "I don't want to keep you waiting up on me."

"Aye, all right, son," Granny Harbinson replied as she bustled out the door. "Mind that kettle doesn't boil over."

Seamus sighed resignedly to himself as he went into the scullery. The way she had replied, he knew his granny wasn't going to pay any heed to him. When he returned that night he would find her keeping her usual vigil at the window, then she'd bolt the front door behind him and splash holy water everywhere. He returned to his seat by the fire when he heard her passing by the front window again. Might as well have a bit of a rest anyway before he went out, he thought; it wouldn't be long till eight o'clock.

That night Granny Harbinson sat by the window, the house in darkness. As the fire flickered shadows around the front room, in the distance she could hear the rattle of gunfire and, closer at hand, the whine of armored pigs as they squealed their way up the Falls Road.

Times hadn't changed much, she reflected, from the years of the '20s when they had to use kidney pavers to force the cage-cars out of the area. Thon was a terrible time. Curfews and martial law, and the Specials arresting all the young men. British soldiers there as well, she recalled, at Paddy Lavery's corner, and sniping coming down from Conway Street. No life for anybody to live, but sure, God was good and they'd come through it all.

She glanced down the street again. The way Minnie Clarke was duking out her window she wasn't intending to remain long in this world, she thought to herself, as she watched Minnie poking her head out the bedroom window. She remembered Minnie the time Joe Devlin's crowd had attacked Donnelly's house. Minnie hadn't been so brave then as the Hibernians smashed windows and splashed paint over Donnelly's door. Poor Missus Donnelly, with her two republican sons in jail and that mob wrecking the only bit of comfort she'd had.

Granny Harbinson—not a granny then of course—had had to face them on her own. She had lost her job as a doffer over that. Her foreman, Ginty McStravick, had been a Hibernian. Ach well, she sighed to herself, she'd outlasted the oul' divil, God rest his soul.

An explosion jarred her thoughts back to Seamus. She wished he was home. Outside, the street fell again as quiet as a grave, the silence punctuated now only by the near-distant echo of pistol and rifle shots.

Forty years ago it had been the same during the Outdoor Relief riots. She smiled as she thought of the fix they'd been in. No money, and seven hungry children to feed. Only they had had unity then, of a sort, until the government had whipped up all the old bitterness and divided the working people.

Another explosion boomed and the windows rattled. She wished Seamus would hurry up. Ah, there he was now. She stirred herself as the key turned in the lock.

"Come in, Seamus son. I fell asleep there saying my prayers so I did. I've a wee mouthful of tea in the pot for you. Drink it up now before you go to bed."

Two or three nights later Seamus asked his granny if he could use the front room. She fussed a little and then took herself off upstairs. She didn't like him using the front. Anybody looking through the window would see them and Minnie Clarke was liable to call at any time. She resolved to warn Seamus about it when his friends weren't there. And they hadn't the wireless turned up. Sure, the people next door would hear the whole commotion. She listened as a scraping noise below the staircase caught her attention. This would have to be the end of it. In future Seamus would have to stick to the back room. All that hammering in the coal-hole. The whole street would hear it. That Seamus one would waken the dead if she wasn't there to keep him in order. The noise stopped. She heard Seamus coming to the foot of the stairs.

"We're away on now, Granny, I'll be in early tonight."

"Wait, Seamus son. . ."

She sighed as she heard the door slamming. Downstairs everything was as normal. She pulled the curtain back from the coal-hole and peered into the space below the stairs. What had that wee lad been doing there?

Groping in the dark, her fingers explored the joists and battens which supported the stairs. A few minutes later, with the help of a breadknife she had the new piece of wood prised off.

"God take care of us," she whispered to herself, "that wee lad needs his bake warmed."

Her heart leapt then, as she heard voices at the door. Who was that now, at this time of the day? Ah, it was only Minnie Clarke. She pushed the wood back into place. She would see Seamus about this some other time.

It was the weekend before she had the chance to get talking to him. She shifted a little in her seat by the window and promised herself that she would have a word with him as soon as he came in. It was quiet tonight, thank God, and as soon as he'd arrive she'd make him a nice cup of tea and have it out with him. The noise of a Saracen in Cape Street made her heart jump. She heard the crashing of gears as it slammed to a halt and then, as another Saracen screamed round from Omar Street, she felt a dryness in the back of her throat.

"Jesus, Mary and Joseph," she whispered, "they're coming here."

It was after midnight when Seamus arrived. He'd heard about the raid from Minnie Clarke. When he came in through the backyard to the scullery his granny fussed about him in her usual fashion.

"Now, Seamus son, no need to worry, everything's all right. Here, get this wee cup o' tea into you. I think you'll have to stay out tonight. Minnie Clarke says you can stay in her house. Now, won't that be. . ."

Seamus swept past her and plunged into the coal-hole. His fingers searched among the joists. He felt sick in the pit of his stomach.

The dump was gone. His hidey-hole was empty. He pulled on the splintered wood and stepped into the front room. His granny had tidied it up a bit but evidence of the raid was still obvious. The settee was ripped, the pictures hung askew and the china cabinet was out from the wall. His granny sat quietly in her usual place by the window. He slumped into a chair by the fire.

"Granny. I had stuff below the stairs and . . . and . . ."

"I know, son."

He sat up as she tugged a package from below her apron. "I didn't like you keeping it there, son. I found it the night you had the meeting in here. I never got around to telling you so I just kept it beneath my corset, so I did. You can't trust nobody nowadays. I kept it on me; it was far safer, son."

Seamus sank back in his seat as his granny shuffled across the room.

"Here you are now."

She handed him the heavy package.

"You'll want to be more careful with that in future, so you will. Will you have your tea now?" She hobbled into the scullery. He heard her poking around the stove.

"God save us, Seamus, but Minnie Clarke nivver came near the house while the soldiers were here. Thon oul' one will nivver change. And you should have seen the many soldiers there was. Peelers too, Seamus, they were everywhere, and me an oul' woman on my own. I gave as good as I took, mind you."

She handed him his tea.

"Now Seamus, son, do you think it will be safe enough for you in Minnie Clarke's?"

Exiles

A PINT OF BITTER, Tom, please." Eamonn Hoban, a fresh-faced man in his early seventies, draped his gangly frame onto a stool at the bar, propped his elbows on the counter and exchanged greetings with the two other customers as he waited for his pint.

The public house consisted of one large room with a bar counter on one side and four snugs on the other. Three or four tables and a corresponding number of chairs filled the floor space and a half-dozen barstools were lined in front of the counter. It was an old-style East London pub. Posters adorning one wall declared the times and venues for set-dancing lessons, a benefit gig for the Birmingham Six and a series of concerts by country-and-western artists.

Eamonn Hoban took a long, appreciative sip at his pint.

"God bless you, Tom," he said finally, setting his glass down on the counter. "I needed that."

He wiped his mouth with the back of his hand and exhaled happily. "I suppose you'll want paid for that." He sighed good-humoredly as he fisted a handful of change onto the counter and arranged it into little silver and copper pillars of coins.

"Indeed I do, Eamonn. Same as always."

"There you are there, all present and correct. Sorry about all the loose change."

"Pass no remarks about that," Tom replied, picking up the money and transferring it to the till. "The more the merrier."

He moved to serve another customer. Eamonn took another, shorter, more contemplative sip of his drink.

"Any word from home?" he asked. The discerning listener would have noticed the soft sing-song west-of-Ireland nuance underscoring his voice.

"Not a word since the last letter I showed you. Have you any news yourself? Anything from Michael?"

"No, I'm not due a letter until next week. He's fine, thank God, according to his last note. He's settled well and still getting plenty of work. And that's half the battle."

"It is, to be sure. The way things are going here, and at home, the man that can get work is a lucky man."

"Had you any word of the Munster Final?"

"Tipp won by two points," one of the other customers chipped in. "Cork threw the game away in the last five minutes. Gave away three frees."

"Ah that was a costly extravagance," Tom made a sour face. "You can't do that at a Munster Final and expect to win. I'll have the video anyway for Thursday night. I'll show it about eight o'clock if ye're interested."

"Indeed and we are," Eamonn enthused. "But I didn't think you'd be anxious now to show such a defeat. Fair play to you," he winked at the others, "you're a real sportsman . . . for a Cork publican."

The other customers joined in the banter. When they had exhausted their collective store of local and regional abuse Eamonn and Tom had their nightly game of draughts. Then, victorious, he had another pint before leaving.

"See you on Thursday night, Tom."

"Right, me oul' son, and if you're writing home don't forget to tell Michael I was asking for him."

"I will indeed. Good night to you all."

His flat was a street away from the pub. He enjoyed the walk. It was a fine night and as he didn't relish the prospect of going indoors so early he strolled to the next corner. It adjoined a busier street with brighter lights, more people and more pubs. He paused for a few minutes, then decided to go to the all-night shop for milk and a packet of biscuits. Since Bridie had died he was always running short of some little thing or other. She would be laughing at him now, going to the shop at this time of night.

Back at the flat he made a bedtime cup of tea, his thoughts turning again to Bridie. It was almost forty years since they had married; forty years in September. They had arrived separately in England, she in May, the year before they wed, from Galway; he, five years earlier from Mayo. He saw her first at Sunday mass in St. Eugene's and they met later that night at the dance organized by Fr. O'Brien in the parish hall. Bridie was in service to a couple who ran a boarding house in Camden. She was lucky: they were an easygoing pair. Other employers would not permit Irish girls time off for mass and dancing; even a night off was out of the question for many in those days. After a week or so he and Bridie started going out together and ten months later they were wed. On their wedding night they resolved to move back to Ireland as soon as they had enough money saved to buy or build a house for themselves. But they never went back, except for wakes or weddings, and as time went on their trips home became more and more associated with mourning or sadness.

They almost stayed a few times. Once especially, when his father had died and they had stayed on a few days longer at the home place to sort things out, he had become wrapped in nostalgia. Memories of childhood flooded back, recollections of his father and the family long locked away were prised loose by his surroundings and by the neighbors' talk, and he had resolved, or almost resolved, that they should stay, modernize the old house, and fulfil their wedding-night resolution. It was not to be. Their own children, Deirdre, Sinead and

Michael, were at school by then, he was in steady work and Bridie was taking in lodgers in the large house they were buying in Islington. When they had talked it over he had had to concede that they had too many commitments. Once, they promised each other again, once they had the house paid off and could sell it at a tidy profit they'd be back. He had even asked his older brother, Brendan, to look out for a half acre somewhere convenient to town, near to the school and shops.

That was twenty years ago. Brendan was long since dead, God rest him, and poor Bridie too. He had buried her only last year.

He didn't bring her home but buried her in their local cemetery at St. Paul's with Sinead, their oldest girl who had been killed in a road accident coming across the city after a late dance. The shock of that had almost destroyed them both. She had been only seventeen; a lovely, laughing daredevil, full of life. In the turmoil of her death they had never considered bringing her back to Ireland. Instead they bought a plot in St. Paul's. When Bridie fell ill and they both knew she was dying she had asked him to bury her with Sinead. And that's what's keeping me here, he reflected sadly as he slipped off to sleep. A grave in an English churchyard and forty years of memories.

On Thursday night after they had watched the video of the Cork–Tipperary match he nursed his pint at his usual place at the bar.

"Are you not yourself?" Tom asked him. "Did you not enjoy the match?"

"I don't know what ails me. It was a grand match. Indeed," he smiled, "it was so good it has made me homesick. I suppose that's what's wrong with me," he continued, brightening up at the thought. "I need to go home, Tom, that's what I need to do."

"It's not a good time for a holiday," Tom reminded him. "February isn't actually the best time of the year for gallivanting around the west of Ireland."

"I'm not talking about a holiday, Tom. I'm talking of going back for good, man dear!"

The Mayo inflections grew with his excitement. "I haven't been back in ten years."

131

"And where would you stay?" Tom asked.

"With Michael, of course!"

"Well, it's none of my business," Tom cautioned, "but I don't think you should rush into anything. Michael's not long back home. He's still got his hands full I'm sure with his new business. And you're not exactly a gossoon. You're settled here. Haven't you a nice flat and doesn't Deirdre come once a week to visit? And," he smiled, "haven't you got me? You'll never get a pint of bitter like this in Newport or Westport or wherever the hell's gates you come from. Fact is, you'll never even get any sort of bitter," he concluded, setting up another pint.

"That's on the house."

"It is?" Eamonn laughed. "Well then, I think I'll buy myself a wee Powers. That's one thing about the English, they stick to what they're good at. Which is why they left us to make the whiskey. Here's *sláinte*, Tom," he raised his glass. "To you and to home."

The next day was Deirdre's regular day to visit him. She changed his bedclothes and fussed around doing her weekly chores as he told her of his plans. Deirdre had never shared her father's or her brother Michael's enthusiasm for Mayo. She liked it well enough for a fortnight every few years. At times she would speak proudly of her roots, but she was a Londoner in every other sense and she had four little children. He couldn't blame her: this was her home. And for all these reasons, she cautioned him as Tom had done, against any hasty decision.

"Daddy, if you want a change I don't see why you won't come and live with us. You know we've always wanted you to—Alan asked you himself. Now, didn't he?" She squared up to him the way her mother often had. It made him smile to see Bridie in her.

"Daddy, you're not even taking me serious. You must be doting to think at your time of life that you can start off afresh again in Ireland. It's not the way it was when you left. Where do you think all your friends are? Where would you stay?"

"I'd stay in Michael's, of course," he replied, emphasizing the "of course" so that she could see the absurdity of her question.

She was not impressed.

"Michael's," she pouted. "Daddy, it's bad enough Michael's away off chasing dreams without you joining him. One fool is enough for any family. Typical men." She softened towards him. "If you went back to live in Ireland when would I see you? I suppose you think I could fly back and forth every week." She laughed. He didn't answer.

"Look, why don't you put off visiting till Patrick's Day," she suggested, "and go over then for a short break and if you still feel the same way, well then fair enough, we'll see about it."

He bristled at her tone.

"I'm not a child, Deirdre, you know!"

"I know that, Daddy," she countered, "but ever since Mammy died you're behaving like one."

The expression on his face told her she had gone too far. She embraced him.

"Oh, Daddy. I'm sorry. I didn't mean to say that. If you want to go home. . ."

He noted with satisfaction that she'd said "home."

"If you want to go, well that's a matter for you. Only don't fall out with me over it. Go for a look first before you finally make up your mind? Please?"

He relented.

"It's the bad oul' Galway blood in you!" he gently scolded her. "That's what gives you the sharp tongue. But I'll do what you ask. For the sake of peace and quiet."

Michael was delighted to see him. He and the children met him at the new airport at Knock and brought him back to a huge and happy feed which Kate had prepared in his honor in the dining room of their new bungalow. They moved the baby out of the back bedroom and put a bed in there for him. Michael took time off work during his first week to drive him around his old haunts. Many had vanished or were vanishing as nature reclaimed derelict cottages and once busy farmyards. He was pleased that the smithy was still recognizable. A Dutch couple were living in the old schoolhouse. They showed him around it and afterwards over coffee they encouraged him to talk of his schooldays. Many of his boyhood friends were dead, more were in England or the U.S.A., he reflected sadly. Those who remained lived miles apart. He'd forgotten how scattered the townland was and how cruel a month March could be.

After the first week Michael was busy again at work, and when it rained Eamonn was confined to the house with Kate and the baby. On the Tuesday of his third week it dawned on him, to his surprise, that all his conversation that morning with her had been about London. The lack of a morning newspaper delivery and the distance to the shop had triggered off his talk.

That evening he told Michael he was going back.

"But I thought you were here for four weeks."

"And so I am, son. But I'm just letting you know I'm going back."

"You're welcome to stay here as long as you like."

"I know, son, and if God spares me, I'll be back whenever I get the chance." He rose from his chair and looked out at the spring evening. A gentle quietness was settling over the mountains. He looked over at Michael with a contented smile.

"Now, seeing as we've that all sorted out, do you think you could spare the time to go down for a pint or two with your oul' fella?"

The rest of his stay was like that. He would spend the day, or most of the day, in the house or, if the weather was fine, he would take a short walk to the school to pick up his grandchildren. In the evening, he and Michael would spend an hour in McAuley's Select Lounge and Public Bar.

One night, as he drifted off to sleep, he smiled to himself as he heard Kate gently chiding Michael over his nightly excursions to the pub. The next day he discreetly arranged for a local girl to babysit and insisted on standing Kate and Michael an evening meal in Westport.

All of this he recounted in lavish detail to Tom on his return to London.

"And what about your plans to return home for good?" Tom asked him mischievously.

"Oh, I'll do that yet," he replied. "It's just a matter of getting Deirdre and Michael used to the idea. You know something,

Tom. . ." He paused to consider the irony of it all. "I only have one son, and when he was growing up I thought of how we'd be able to spend a bit of time together when he was older. Now he's back in Ireland far from where he was reared and I'm here in London, far from where I was reared. Isn't that a strange state of affairs?"

He paused again. Tom waited for him to continue.

"Some of the younger ones call our Michael's the English family. The older ones," he finished proudly, "the older ones call him Eamonn Hoban's son."

"It's good that there's Hobans back there again," Tom remarked.

"Aye, that's what I was thinking myself. You never know what's before you, that's what Bridie used always say." He paused. "But at least some of us made it back.

"Now, when I go back for keeps," he dipped his face into his pint so that Tom couldn't tell if he was serious or not, "when I go back I'd need a place of me own. Mind you, our Michael's is great but there's nothing like your own place. I've got used to my bit of independence. When I get that sorted out then you could come and spend the weekend of the Munster Final with me, couldn't you? Páirc Uí Chaoimh or Thurles." He looked at Tom over his glass. "That's if Cork ever make it that far again."

"Oh they will, Eamonn. They will, but I doubt you and I will watch it here on the video." He smiled.

Eamonn was taken aback. "Ah now, man dear, don't be so sure of that. But giv's another pint and pull one for yourself. The next one I buy you will be in McAuley's. Only it'll be Guinness instead of this oul' bitter, and Guinness like it should be, not the way they serve it here. Then you'll know what a real pint is. Okay, Tom?"

"Whatever you say, Eamonn. Whatever you say."

Tom set the two pints on the counter and Eamonn and he raised their glasses to one another.

"Here's to the Munster Final," he smiled.

"To us and the Munster Final," Eamonn corrected him.

"To us," Tom agreed, "and the Munster Final."

Of Mice and Men

I T WAS HUGH DEENEY who suggested that the mouse should have a fair trial. Hugh was like that, cautious and judicial and fair-minded about most things. Except women, maybe, but that's another story.

The mouse in question had dropped in on Hugh one morning while he was eating his breakfast porridge. And when I say dropped in, I mean that quite literally: it fell from the timbers which constituted a ceiling-cum-roof in the political prisoners' quarters. With a dull, wet plop it dropped into Hugh's porridge-bowl. The porridge probably saved its life. Luckily it wasn't hot, but prison porridge is never hot. Hugh was nearly as shocked as the mouse and, in a reflex action I suppose, he cupped his hands over the bowl. The mouse, half drowned, concussed and winded, was captured. Then Hugh gave the mouse—and us—a second shock. As the mouse pulled itself together and peered upwards Hugh opened his fingers a crack and peered down. Their eyes met. The mouse may have screamed, no one knows; but if it did its cry was drowned by Hugh's long shrill wail of a shriek.

"There's a mouse in my porridge," he squealed. "It fell from wah-hhhhh. . ."

The rest of his utterance was lost in an almost hysterical keen.

Hugh's comrades responded to his trouble in their usual supportive, stoical way.

"Ah, meat at last," someone smirked.

"Everybody'll want one now," the hut OC complained.

"I hate mieces to pieces," snarled Cleaky.

"It's alive," Hugh finally stammered, his hands still clasped over the bowl.

"Kill the bastard," snarled his bosom buddy, Gerry Skelly.

"Kill the bastard," ordered the hut OC.

"Kill him," rose the chorus.

Hugh had by now regained his composure.

"Hold on, hold on," he pleaded. "This mouse deserves a fair trial."

"Kill him!" shouted Joe Ryan, advancing towards Hugh and his porridge-bowl captive.

"I captured him," Hugh announced defiantly.

"Captured him!" Joe scoffed. "You're lucky it wasn't a fair fight: that mouse would have ate and shit you. Captured him! The poor mouse surrendered."

He moved towards Hugh again.

"Stay back, Joe, I'm warning you. Stay back! Back off!"

Hugh commanded the mob. "If you don't back off I'll let him go. He deserves a fair crack of the whip."

"Stop!" the hut OC yelled. "Okay," he smiled crookedly at Hugh, "your mouse'll have his day in court. There will be a staff meeting at twelve to appoint the court. You can nominate the defense and the court will commence proceedings in the half-hut after visits this afternoon. Okay?"

"*Maith go leor*,"* Hugh agreed.

By the time the court assembled at five o'clock, the half-hut was packed tight with spectators. Indeed the hut OC had to call for

---

* Fair enough

*ciúnas** three times before the hubbub of noise receded. Then he informed the assembled mass that an incident had occurred that morning during which a mouse had been captured alive. It was, he went on, as everyone knew, camp policy to kill all mice on account of the damage they did and the risk to health they constituted. Heretofore the mice had neither given nor had they expected any quarter. Despite this, the comrade who captured the mouse had refused to kill the offending creature. Here the OC paused and looked at Hugh for a long, sneer-filled second or two.

"So," he continued patiently, "I consulted with the proper authorities regarding procedure, the rights of defendants and so on and so forth, and in my capacity as convener I have appointed a three-person tribunal and a prosecutor. Hugh Deeney has nominated himself to act in defense of the mouse."

Hugh permitted himself a curt little nod towards the body of the court. The OC ignored him and continued his speech.

"Now, I have only a few little formalities to oversee and I will turn the court over to the Presiding Officer. I would ask the Presiding Officer, Mr. Gerry Skelly, to take his seat along with the other members of the tribunal, Mr. Moby McAteer and wee Jimmy Drain. I would also ask Mr. Clarke the Prosecutor to take his seat and as for Mr. Deeney and the mouse, I would ask that they present themselves before the court."

Two tables had been set end to end for the tribunal of judges. At right angles to them and facing each other two single tables were set up for the prosecutor and defense. When all concerned were seated in their appointed places the OC faced the court again.

"I have to establish first whether the defendant has agreed to his defense counsel." Here a snigger rippled through the courtroom. "And then I have to ask you all to pledge yourselves to conduct these proceedings in a fair and just manner. This court will be a military tribunal, as befits the status of the captured enemy. Its verdict will be guilty or death—I mean, not guilty or death," he hurriedly corrected

---

* silence

himself. "There will be no appeal."

"Now," he addressed Hugh. "Has the defendant agreed that you should act on his behalf?"

"In so far as I can establish, yes," Hugh confirmed. "And anyway," he stammered earnestly, "you do have the right to appoint the defense and I would request that you do so by ratifying my appointment." He bowed graciously.

Some of the rowdier elements in the court applauded and the OC permitted himself a good-humored grin.

"Fair enough," he said. "Now I want you all to rise."

"A point of order please," Hugh interrupted. "The defense has the right to object to members of the tribunal?"

"Well, yes, I suppose so."

"Well," Hugh hurried on, making the most of his advantage, "I want to object to the Presiding Officer and I ask for an adjournment till tomorrow so that I can present my case."

"Are you serious?" The OC was flabbergasted.

"Yes, my client's life is at stake."

"For fuck sake!"

Hugh was unabashed. "I've made my point," he said.

"Why don't you refuse to recognize the court?" a voice from the back called out.

"Order!" commanded the OC.

"Is my request granted?" Hugh persisted politely.

"Well, I suppose so," came the grudging reply. "Till the marra then, same time. The court will now rise."

And so, with a great clatter of noise, of seats scraping backwards on the floor, of voices raised and doors slamming, the court adjourned.

* * *

"Therefore the purpose of this court cannot be fulfilled unless each of the judges is unbiased and without prejudice and is seen to be so."

As Hugh concluded his opening remarks the court was hanging on his every word. His submission had been masterful, unusually brief and understated.

"I think it goes without saying that all of us are in total agreement on that point," the OC snapped testily at him.

Hugh looked at him benignly.

"Mr. Convener, have I permission to question the panel?"

The OC nodded.

"Thank you."

"M'lud," a voice from the back added.

Hugh faced Gerry Skelly.

"Mr. Skelly, did you, on the morning that my client was captured, did you incite others to murder him?"

"Objection!" the prosecutor intervened.

"Yes?" said the OC.

"I object to the words incite and murder. Also, if I may say so, the court has not established the sex of the mouse."

"Sustained."

"Did you or did you not, shout 'kill the bastard'?" Hugh faced Gerry Skelly indignantly.

Skelly smirked. "I don't have to answer that."

"Oh yes you do," Hugh barked.

Skelly's smirk widened. "Oh no I don't." He stood up and, waving his arms at the body of the court, he encouraged the spectators to join him in chorus.

"Oh no you don't," they bayed.

Hugh screamed to be heard above the uproar.

"Contempt of court! This outburst has proved my case. I move for a change of Presiding Officer."

As the noise subsided he smiled in triumph.

"Okay," the OC smiled back at him. "Wee Jimmy Drain will be Presiding Officer." He paused for effect. "And Gerry Skelly will be prosecutor. . ." he waved Hugh's objections aside, "and I hereby declare this court properly convened. Thank you, Mr. Drain."

He bowed slightly to wee Jimmy, who had changed places with Skelly.

"This court is now in session," wee Jimmy announced. "Mr. Skelly will open the case for the prosecution."

140

"No problem," Gerry began. "This case isn't really about a mouse. It is about whether we all agree to abide by the rules of this camp. Our rules. It is just an accident that the rule in dispute here is about a mouse: it could be about anything. For example, it could be about visits. We have rules about visits; our rules, not the screws' rules. And those rules, like the ones about mice, are for the common good. If we go around breaking them just when the fancy takes us then where would we be, eh?"

He looked around the court for approval.

"Hugh doesn't like the rule about mice. Or maybe it's just this particular mouse. We don't know," he sneered, "do we? So he decides to break the rules. Fair enough, you may think. We're all broadminded; easy come, easy go. But just say Hugh, or somebody else for that matter, just say they don't like the rules about visits. Should they just do their own thing? Eh? Then where would we be? We wouldn't know our arse from our elbow, would we?"

The court was deadly quiet.

"We would have a state of anarchy wouldn't we? And how would we explain that to our wives and mothers and girlfriends? How could we explain that Hugh or somebody else was getting all the visits. Just because he didn't like the rules! We couldn't, could we? So this isn't about the mouse. It's about us. It's about how we want to conduct ourselves. And in order for us to do so properly, in a way that makes things easy for us all, requires all of us to accept a certain responsibility to keep the rules."

He looked around the court again.

"The rules about mice are straightforward. Mice are the enemy. Mice carry disease. Mice destroy our belongings. Mice eat our food. So what do we do?"

His voice was heavy with sarcasm.

"Do we talk to the mice? Sign treaties with them? Perhaps in the past someone did try all those things. Who knows? If they did, it didn't work. So it was decided that the mice had to be destroyed: that did work. The mice got the message. Yous have heard about the old days when the mice overran this place. Is that what yous want? That's why we have rules: for our own good. And that's why we should keep them: for our own good. And that's why this court can deliver only one verdict. For our own good."

As he sat down, face flushed and intense, a murmur of applause whispered through the court.

Hugh got slowly to his feet. He smiled over towards Skelly.

"I see my comrade is taking this a bit more seriously than he'd like to admit. I never thought I'd hear him sounding off in such an authoritarian manner. And, of course, as we used to say about Joe Stalin, there's a lot you'd agree with."

"The mouse is a Trot," someone guffawed.

"Nawh, it's a Maoist. Mousey Tung."

Even Skelly and Hugh allowed themselves a smile as the court erupted in laughter. When order was restored Hugh continued his submission.

"But it's how you apply the rules that's important. There are very few really bad rules. It's how they're interpreted that makes the difference. I'm not arguing against the rules: I'm not even arguing against the rules about mice. I know and I accept why we have those rules. So all the things my comrade said are a diversion. You see, he left one thing out. What was that you may ask? Well, it's a bit hard to explain precisely in words but yous all know what I mean, don't yous? Common sense, compassion, the right to use our discretion: that's what he left out. We don't just apply or follow rules blindly. And if I may say so, if we did the first person to object—and fair play to him—would be my old friend Skelly. So he's fooling no one with all that high-sounding rhetoric. No, this isn't about rules. This is about how we apply them. It isn't academic either or for a bit of *craic*. My client's life is at stake. Aye, yous can smile if yous like but it's no laughing matter as far as I'm concerned."

Hugh's eyes swept the court. Smiles and smirks faded before his relentless gaze.

"Nawh, lads, this is serious. Okay, it might be just a mouse and so what, you may say. Fair enough. But not all mice are the same." Someone in the middle of the court started to snigger. Hugh glared and the snigger died away as the culprit wilted, red-faced and embarrassed, before him.

"This mouse fell among us by accident. He wasn't even trespassing. There is no proof that he presented any threat to any of us. As far as we know he was minding his own business on his own territory when he fell into our hut. Now, if he had been in somebody's food-locker or among our clothes or even scampering about the floor I wouldn't even try to make a case, but he was doing none of these things. So what's he guilty of? Nothing. Nothing except being a mouse and that's hardly his fault, is it?"

"It is not," wee Jimmy Drain whispered, almost to himself.

The OC and Gerry Skelly stared at him in disbelief. Wee Jimmy recovered his composure.

"Is that the end of your submission?"

"Aye," Hugh replied, "I rest my case."

He sat down with an air of satisfaction. He had obviously won wee Jimmy over to his side and as Presiding Officer wee Jimmy had a casting vote. Things looked good for him and the mouse. He lifted the cardboard shoebox which held the defendant. The court prepared to rise.

It was then that Gerry Skelly cried out: "Hold on! I have the right to make a final submission. Am I going to be denied that right?"

"No, of course not," said Jimmy testily. "Say your piece."

"I won't be long," Gerry replied sweetly. "I won't be long because what I have to say will only take a minute. My learned friend here," he gestured towards Hugh, "my learned friend here rests his entire case on the assertion that his mouse is an innocent bystander who has mysteriously dropped into our midst. He offers no explanation or evidence for this. And do yous know why? Because he knows the terrible truth. That mouse is a paratrooper, that's what he is! He didn't fall from the roof, he parachuted in on us!"

Gerry finished in triumph, pointing at Hugh and his little cardboard shoebox.

"A bloody paratrooper!" he repeated.

Hugh's face fell.

Someone at the back shouted "Kill the bastard!"

Hugh clutched the shoebox to his chest. He heard the mouse scraping inside.

"Have you anything to say?" wee Jimmy asked.

Hugh shook his head.

"This court will now adjourn to consider its verdict. A majority verdict will suffice," wee Jimmy announced. He avoided Hugh's gaze. "The prisoner has to be put into the custody of the Cage authority. The court will now rise."

The panel of judges left to consider their verdict. Hugh got slowly to his feet as the Cage OC approached to take custody of the mouse. As he did so Hugh stumbled. It was obviously a contrived stumble, awkwardly and amateurishly executed. The mouse's box fell from his grasp. It bounced onto the table and fell to the floor. The OC made a Herculean effort to catch it, but he failed. The shoebox burst open and the mouse scampered free.

Pandemonium reigned. The mouse darted towards the body of the court, the door beyond it and freedom. His escape route was blocked by a mob of squealing, screaming men. He darted back again, back towards Hugh and then, turning suddenly, made another valiant charge at the mob. Hugh yelled encouragement.

The mouse stopped again, disoriented by the noise. He turned once more but too late! A size ten Doc Martin boot descended on him and he was stomped, savagely and repeatedly, underfoot.

Hugh let out a long, anguished scream of rage and flung himself towards the culprits. It was a full three minutes before things settled down. It took two men to restrain Hugh but eventually order was restored.

The panel of judges returned. The OC tried to tell wee Jimmy that the mouse was dead, but wee Jimmy wouldn't let him talk.

"We have reached our decision," he shouted down the hut, before turning towards where Hugh sat. "The mouse is innocent. By a majority vote we find him not guilty as charged. Set him free."

Wee Jimmy smiled at Hugh. It was the smile, the happy, inno-cently compassionate smile, which comes to the lips of the doer of a good deed. It was a smile of quiet self-satisfaction, of inner content-ment, of a man who surprised himself by doing the noble thing, and making the right decision. Wee Jimmy was pleased because he knew Hugh had faith in him. Wee Jimmy had kept that faith. He was pleased because he knew Hugh also would be pleased. He had lived up to Hugh's belief in him. Wee Jimmy smiled his smile again at Hugh.

Hugh stared blankly back at him. Then he lifted the empty shoe-box and without a word he walked out of the hut.

Also available from Roberts Rinehart Publishers

Long before he became President of Sinn Féin, Gerry Adams was a civil rights activist who led sit-ins, marches and protests in Northern Ireland. Along with hundreds of other men, Adams was interned on the Maidstone prison ship and in Long Kesh prison—without charge or trial—during the 1970s for his political activities. *Cage Eleven* is his own account—sometimes passionate, often humorous—of life in Long Kesh. Written while Adams was a prisoner, the pieces were smuggled out for publication.

ISBN 1-57098-131-0 $12.95

Falls Memories: A Belfast Life

This nostalgic and very personal account of a working-class Irish community abounds with light-hearted humor.

ISBN 1-879373-96-3   10.95

Free Ireland: Toward a Lasting Peace

Adams' personal statement on the meaning, importance, and inspiration of modern Irish republicanism.

ISBN 1-879373-95-5 $11.95

To order these titles or for a catalog of Roberts Rinehart publications, please write or fax:

Roberts Rinehart Publishers
5455 Spine Road
Boulder, Colorado 80305
Tel. 800.352.1985 Fax. 303.530.4488